PUFFIN BOOKS

Wyvern Fall

[...] Forward was born in Coventry. He went to college to [pur]sue theological training and subsequently became a p[...] priest. He is now a full-time writer and lives with his [wife a]nd two daughters near Hull.

M[ich]ael Foreman is one of the leading children's ill[ustr]ators working today. He has won numerous [pre]gious awards, including the Smarties Grand Prix prize [19]94 for *War Game*. He spends his time with his wife [and s]ons partly in London and partly at his house in St [Ive]s, Cornwall.

Wyvern Fall

Toby Forward

Illustrated by Michael Foreman

PUFFIN BOOKS

PUFFIN BOOKS

Published by the Penguin Group
Penguin Books Ltd, 27 Wrights Lane, London W8 5TZ, England
Penguin Books USA Inc., 375 Hudson Street, New York, New York 10014, USA
Penguin Books Australia Ltd, Ringwood, Victoria, Australia
Penguin Books Canada Ltd, 10 Alcorn Avenue, Toronto, Ontario, Canada M4V 3B2
Penguin Books (NZ) Ltd, 182–190 Wairau Road, Auckland 10, New Zealand

Penguin Books Ltd, Registered Offices: Harmondsworth, Middlesex, England

First published by Andersen Press Limited 1994
Published in Puffin Books 1996
1 3 5 7 9 10 8 6 4 2

For Bill Charlton
with much love and many thanks

My goode myn, noot I for-why ne how
That jalousie, allas! that wikked wyvere,
Thus causeles is cropen into yow,
The harm of which I wolde fayn delyvere.
Allas, that he, al hool, or of him slyvere,
Shuld han his refut in so digne a place,
Ther Jove hym soone out of youre herte arace!

(Geoffrey Chaucer – *Troilus and Criseyde*)

ONE

The trouble started the day that Weever announced that there would be no Harvest Thanksgiving in the village. So, of course, they blamed him.

He was an easy man to blame. Huge, with flowing black hair, a beard and fierce eyes, he had been the vicar for less than two years, so he was viewed as an outsider in Herpeton.

'There's always been a Harvest,' Mrs Reeves

9

complained.

'Always?' Weever raised heavy eyebrows at her with a mocking glance.

'It's tradition. Hundreds of years.'

Weever laughed out loud.

'No such thing,' he said.

She grew pink-faced. 'Are you calling me a liar?'

Thomas looked on at the scene with interest and some amusement. He didn't like Weever either, but there was always some pleasure to be had from seeing two grown-ups argue. He was slightly disappointed when Weever seemed to be backing down, but then he was pleased when the priest really savaged Mrs Reeves.

'Not a liar,' he said. 'Of course not. I wouldn't dream of saying such a thing.' Mrs Reeves smiled, briefly.

'Just ignorant,' Weever added.

The row that followed was wonderful to Thomas's ears. He scratched Towser's smooth chest and ran his fingers through the silky sandy hair.

Mrs Reeves's piggy little eyes grew smaller and smaller as she became crosser and crosser. Weever's manner grew more and more patient and helpful as his words became ruder and ruder.

'So you see,' he finished, 'the first Harvest Thanksgiving in England was only a hundred and fifty years ago. 1843. In Cornwall. And it must have taken a bit of time to find its way up here. So, it's hardly traditional. Hardly been going on in Herpeton for hundreds of years.'

Mrs Reeves squirmed with anger. 'You're making it up,' she said.

'Oh, no,' Weever assured her. 'I wouldn't do that. It really is new. Even Thanksgiving Day in America is older. Isn't that so, Miss Aylmer?'

Felicity Aylmer, who had been arranging flowers and pretending not to listen, turned her head towards them. 'I guess so.'

'There'll be trouble,' Mrs Reeves warned the priest. 'Big trouble. You mark my words.'

'Why do you say that?' asked Miss Aylmer, suddenly interested.

Mrs Reeves looked uncomfortable. 'I don't know,' she said. 'I just feel it. Doing away with tradition. It's sure to cause trouble.'

'But Saint Romanus' Day. That's traditional. That's what we'll have instead. October 23rd.'

'Over my dead body,' Mrs Reeves snapped. And she swung the heavy wooden door shut behind her as she stormed out.

'I hope not,' said Weever.

But it nearly was.

Mrs Reeves was so angry that she rode her bicycle straight out in front of a car. The road was slippery with mud and rain. The car braked, and, luckily, skidded away from her. But it still caught the front wheel of her bike and sent her spinning round, off the road, into the fence. The

11

last thing she saw, as her bike flicked from underneath her, was the open mouth of the bronze wyvern weather vane, perched on its globe above the spire. It seemed to be laughing at her. Then it twisted in the autumn winds.

Afterwards, in hospital, she said that the worst thing was the sound of her leg as it snapped.

'It didn't hurt at all,' she told everyone. 'Not at the time, that is. It does now.' And she pulled a long-suffering face and pointed to the plaster-of-Paris that stretched out in front of her. 'But the snap was something terrible.'

And then she would lower her voice and tell the visitor how Weever had threatened her with harm just before she left the church. 'Over my dead body,' she said. Which wasn't quite the truth, but it was how she remembered it, so it wasn't exactly a lie. And people didn't quite believe her, but the story stuck, and so they came to feel more uncomfortable than ever with Weever.

As the time for the Saint Romanus celebrations drew nearer, more and more accidents happened. And Weever found himself blamed for most of them. Feeling in the village grew against him, and when Mrs Reeves said, as she often did, 'He doesn't belong here. I wish he'd go back to where he came from,' she spoke for quite a lot of them.

As for Weever, he was uncomfortable about the

bad feeling, but he was determined not to give way, even when the accidents became too much to ignore.

Thomas hurried from the church just in time to see Mrs Reeves hit the fence. The excitement of the screeching brakes and the broken leg, the ambulance and the small crowd kept him warm in the September afternoon. But when it was all over and the flashing blue lights disappeared, he shuddered in his coat, whistled to Towser and ran home across the village green.

His mother tutted at him.

'Should know better than to stand gawping at an accident.'

'I was only trying to help.'

'Hmm.' She sounded doubtful. 'And did you?'

'No. They wouldn't let me.'

He grabbed a toasted crumpet and bit into it. Towser curled up in front of the fire.

'Letter for you,' said Mrs Ketch. 'On the mantelpiece.'

Thomas took the envelope and turned it over and over in his hands, putting a buttery thumbprint on it. 'It's from Clare,' he said.

'Oh, yes.'

The flimsy air mail paper, and the stamp with the koala on it had already told her.

Thomas stuffed it into his pocket.

'Aren't you going to read it?'

'Later.'

She poured his tea and smiled. 'Just like a Ketch.'

'What do you mean?'

'Always secrets. Nothing's ever straight-forward with you. Not even a letter.'

Thomas chewed his crumpet.

'Will she be all right?' he asked.

'Clare?'

'Mrs Reeves.'

'You know better than I do.'

'She was talking a lot when they carried her off.'

'That's always a good sign.'

'I'll go upstairs.'

Towser bounded ahead of Thomas, up the twisting wooden stairs. The cottage was very old and low and cosy in the autumn dusk.

Thomas sat on his bed and carefully slit the letter open with his penknife.

'It's from Clare,' he told Towser.

Towser put his head to one side and listened.

'Dear Thomas,' the boy read out loud.

'It's taken us *months* to get here. The ship stopped in Africa and India, and Singapore, and some islands before we got to Australia. I was sick seventeen times. Fifteen times because of the sea and once because of bad food, and once because I ate ice cream and fresh mango and a hot dog all at the same time. Jack says it serves

14

me right, but I don't care because I was so used to throwing up by then that it didn't matter. He was sick more than me when the ship rolled.

'He made me promise not to tell you that he cried when he looked at the photograph of Towser the other day. Are you looking after him?'

Thomas looked up. 'Am I?' he asked. Towser ignored the question.

Thomas read on.

'Jack says he wishes he'd never left Towser behind, but he couldn't have come with us, so that's stupid.

'The weather here is really hot. I bet you're shivering.

'Our house has got a verandah and blinds and a huge garden with such funny plants and trees in it. And Dad says there are poisonous spiders, so we have to be careful.

'Dad has started his new job and Mum is making cups and bowls out of pottery and selling them in a shop.

'We start our new school next week.

'Please write soon and tell me all the news.

'Have you caught a wyvern yet?

Your friend,
Clare.'

Thomas folded the letter, put it carefully back in the envelope and tapped it gently on Towser's nose.

'You can forget Jack,' he said. 'You're my dog now.'

He found a notepad and a pen.

Towser put a damp noseprint on the paper.

'Ugh,' said Thomas. He tore it off and crumpled it up. Towser did it again.

Thomas sighed. 'Is that your message?' he asked.

Towser wagged his tail.

'All right.' Thomas drew a circle round it and wrote: 'Towser's letter.' Then he started his own.

'Dear Clare,

Thank you for your letter. You have had a good time. Hardly anything has happened here.'

He blew his nose, to help him to think what to write next.

'Except that there was an American girl here in the summer, just after you left, with her dad. She disappeared, and when she was found again she had been through a secret entrance under Stone Pond. It took her to another world where the wyverns come from. And she met a boy called the Kych, who was just like me, and a man like Weever, with a dragon tattoo on his arm. And a girl, who was just like old Miss Aylmer, only a girl. And the boy and the man had tattoos on their arms, just like the snake tattoos that Weever and Miss Aylmer have got.

'Anyway, she had all sorts of adventures, and you'll never guess what. She brought back a key with her. Like the one we were looking for. And a bottle of medicine that made Mum better. So it's all all right now.

'And she brought the book, Thomas Kych's book. The one we've been looking for. I was really excited, because it would tell us how to make the wyverns fly, and to be able to call them whenever we wanted to. But the thing is, that she said, the girl said, that she could read it when she was in that world, but when we looked in it it wasn't in English, or in any language anyone could read. But it doesn't mean anything to us. Weever spends all his time trying to read it, but he doesn't do any good. So we still can't make the wyverns fly, and I want that more than anything else in the world.'

Thomas sat back and stretched. His arm ached from writing. And he felt a bit dizzy from thinking so hard and trying to get everything right for Clare. He read it through. Then he carried on.

'It was really strange, knowing that there's a boy just like me only in another world. And . . .'

Thomas hesitated. Then he wrote, but more slowly, thinking hard.

'The thing is, I think that Miss Aylmer, and Weever and me, we all come from through there. Not us, I mean, but our great-great-grand-parents. I think they came through and got stuck here. So, really I don't belong here. I belong there. It's a really strange feeling.'

17

Towser snuffed at Thomas and Thomas stopped to scratch the dog's ears.

'And something's happening in the village,' he continued. 'Mrs Reeves was run over today. And I just know there will be other things. I think the wyverns want to go back. I think we've started something and it hasn't finished yet. And I think I want to go back.'

Thomas read through what he had written and scored a line through the last sentence.

'I don't want to go back,' he said to Towser. 'Do I?'

Towser licked him.

'I've always been here.'

He read the letter again, then he crumpled it up.

'Dear Clare,' he wrote. 'Thank you for your letter. What an exciting time you have had. Things have been very dull here without you and Jack. I expect you will soon feel as though you have always lived in Australia and you will forget about us. Please keep in touch with
Your friend,
Thomas.'

'She's already forgotten that the wyverns are real, she'd laugh at me,' he explained to Towser.

Towser huddled up to Thomas.

'So, I'm on my own now,' Thomas said. 'But I will make them fly. I will. I can.'

He looked at the bedroom door, to check that

they were not being watched, then he pushed up the sleeve of his pullover. 'Look,' he said. Towser pushed a wet nose on the boy's arm, just where the blue pattern was beginning to appear.

A thick fist beat loudly on the front door of the cottage, and Thomas jumped. He pushed his sleeve down quickly.

'Can I speak to Thomas?' The voice sounded near enough to be in his room. Though the cottage was small it needed a huge voice to carry that well.

'Weever,' said Thomas. 'I hate him. Don't let him in,' he begged his mother silently.

Her voice made a soft answer. The door closed. Then, louder, she called up the stairs.

'Thomas. You've got a visitor.'

TWO

'Shouldn't you be at the hospital?' said Thomas.

'Don't be rude,' said his mother.

Weever gave a wide grin. 'I've rung them,' he said. 'She'll be all right. And I can't see her while she's having her leg set. I'll go round later.'

Thomas kept his eyes away from Weever's.

'I don't want to talk to you,' he said.

'Thomas! If you can't mend your manners you'll go straight to bed,' his mother warned him.

'I'd rather he didn't,' said Weever. 'I would like to talk to him.'

'Not here,' said Thomas.

'My house, then,' suggested Weever.

'No,' said Thomas.

'Afraid?' asked Weever. His huge head flew back, and he gave a yelp of laughter.

'No!'

'Come on then.'

Weever stepped through the door and into the cold evening air.

Thomas hesitated, but when Towser darted after the black figure Thomas followed.

The vicarage was behind the church, and they had to cross the village green to reach it. The empty shape of Wivern Manor, the great house, glowered down at them through the gloom. The windows were boarded up. The doors were nailed shut. The iron gates were fastened with a thick chain and padlock. On each gatepost a stone dragon crouched, wings ready to fly, tail curved, talons digging into the round support on which it perched.

Weever ignored them. Thomas looked carefully, half expecting them to fly off as they had once, nearly a year before.

Weever's cassock flapped in the strong wind and he pulled it up a little to prevent it dragging in the mud.

Towser leaped ahead, enjoying the autumn

gusts. He waited for them, and grinned up at the blind face of the statue of the Lady of the Manor, Jane Gwyer, in the middle of the green. Thomas put a hand on Towser's neck and followed the line of his eyes.

'What happened to her?' he asked Weever.

'It tells you on the plinth,' the man said, sharply. 'She disappeared, hundreds of years ago.'

'But you know, don't you?' said Thomas.

'Better get in before the rain starts,' said Weever.

Thomas had never been inside the vicarage, and he didn't know anyone who had. For many years it had stood empty, but when Weever arrived he refused to live in the new house the last vicar had lived in, and he moved into the old one, using his own money to do the jobs needed to make it safe to live in. He used the modern vicarage for meetings, but slept in the old house. Right until the last moment, Thomas hoped that they would go to the bright new house, but he had always known that it was a vain wish. They passed the church, took the path through the graveyard and made towards the old house.

Weever took a bunch of keys from his deep pocket and selected the largest one. He swung open his gate and Towser scampered ahead. Thomas watched the man slam the gate shut. Ahead of them, the vicarage stood waiting. Dark

and silent, brooding over them, it was built of
grey stone, with pointed windows, like a church,
and a wide wooden door, on elaborate hinges,
with a brass sign – 'Saint Romanus' vicarage'.
An iron knocker hung on the middle of the door.
Thomas looked at it closely, thinking at first it
was a decorated metal ring, but he eventually
made out that its shape was that of a wyvern, a
two-legged, winged dragon, curled round, with
its tail in its own mouth. He shuddered.

'Did you put this here?' he asked, fearing that
it was an ancient device, with some sort of
meaning.

'Yes,' said Weever. He threw the door open. It
had not been locked. He saw the relief register
on Thomas's face. 'I found it in the crypt,' he
said. 'It's very old.' He laughed at the return of
Thomas's unease, and the roar echoed through
the great hall and up the stairs.

'After you,' Weever invited Thomas.

The hall was as menacing as the outside of the
house: stone-flagged floor; walls panelled in dark
wood; a high ceiling and a flight of stairs that
curved out of sight. It was cold, gloomy and
unwelcoming.

'I don't get many visitors,' said Weever.

'I'm not surprised,' said Thomas, glad that his
mother wasn't there to hear him cheek Weever.

The man grabbed the handle of an inner door.
'We'll go in here,' he said.

Harry Dobbs poked the end of his walking stick in the cold ashes of the Green Dragon. The village pub had burned down a few months earlier.

'Looking for something, Harry?'

'Nothing I'm likely to find.'

Ted Ketch picked his way carefully over the burned ground, making sure his footing was safe on the tumbled brickwork and twisted iron.

'And what might that be?' he asked. 'A pint of usual?'

Harry did not return the man's cheerful smile. But Ted didn't mind that. No one could remember ever having seen Harry smile, so they expected no sign of whether he was cheerful or disgruntled.

'I can do without a drink,' he said.

'Good job.'

'Not that I wouldn't mind one.'

Ted waited.

'Should be fenced off, this,' said Harry.

'Wouldn't stop people poking about,' said Ted. 'Not if they wanted to.'

'Could burst into flames again,' said Harry.

'Not much chance.'

'What do you know?' the old man demanded, suddenly angry.

'At least two months since it burned down. And I saw them pump thousands of gallons of water on here. Four days. And they pulled up the floors and pumped more into the cellars. There's not a

24

dry spot, not a glowing coal here.'

'Huh!'

'But you're right in one way,' Ted agreed, peaceably.

'What's that?'

'It isn't safe. Ground's uneven. You could trip. The cellars go all over, underground. There could be subsidence. We could fall through.'

Harry moved forward, scraping his stick through the ashes.

'You looking for something?' asked Ted.

Harry trod carefully. 'That boy of yours,' he said at last.

'What about him?'

'He's over to the vicar's house.'

And Harry pointed his stick at the old vicarage, to make sure Ted did not mistake him.

'He'll be all right there,' said Ted.

'All right! All right! Are you puddled?' Harry glared at Thomas's father. 'Weevers and Ketches don't mix. You know that.'

'I don't know,' said Ted. 'There's never been a Weever here before.'

A look of angry disgust passed over Harry's face. 'There's always been Weevers here.'

'Not in my time,' said Ted. 'Nor in yours.'

'Don't give me that,' said Harry. 'I know. I'm Old Herpeton. And you are. There's been Ketches and Dobbs here as long as anyone knows. And Weevers,' he added.

'So they say,' agreed Ted.

'And I'll tell you what,' said Harry. 'I'll tell you for nothing – Weevers and Ketches don't get on. Never did. Never will.'

'They say that, too,' said Ted. 'But he seems all right to me.'

Harry snorted. 'I wouldn't let my boy in that house with a Weever,' he said. 'Not if I was a Ketch.'

Ted took Harry's arm. 'Come on. You'll fall over.'

Harry gave the grimace that did duty for a smile on his face. 'I've never fallen over in the Green Dragon yet,' he said. 'And I doubt I will when there's no ale to serve.'

Ted laughed at the joke.

They were picking their way across the rubble together when they heard the whoosh of the flames, and smelt the smoke.

Behind them, just where Harry had been standing, a column of fire rose up against the sky.

Thomas gasped when he saw the room.

'Come on in,' said Miss Aylmer.

She sat in a deep armchair in front of a crackling fire.

Instead of the cold, dank chamber that Thomas had expected he found himself walking into a bright, warm, and splendidly decorated room.

The ceiling, high and white, was embossed with swirling patterns picked out in red and gold. The walls were covered with green and red paper, and the windows hung about with rich crimson curtains. Despite the riot of colour Thomas found the room restful and welcoming. There was no central light, but the room was lit by a number of lamps, and there was a tall candelabrum in one corner, with many branches, each one topped with a real, guttering candle. Its feet were claws and its holders were open dragon's mouths. The stem, Thomas finally made out, was a twisted serpent's body.

Weever looked pleased with himself.

'Everything ready, Felicity?' he asked.

'You brought him, then,' said Miss Aylmer.

'He was nervous,' Weever laughed.

'I was not,' Thomas argued.

Towser sniffed at the feet of the candelabrum.

'Have some punch,' she offered Thomas. She ladled a hot drink from a silver bowl which was heated by the fire.

Weever poured a whiskey, flung himself into another armchair and watched Thomas, who chose a seat on a sofa, and did not taste his drink.

'It's poison,' Weever explained to him.

Thomas tried to smile.

Miss Aylmer poured herself a cup from the same bowl, and drank it.

'What have we got?' Weever suddenly demanded.

'Eh?' said Thomas.

Weever stood up again and paced the large room, his cassock flowing behind him, the glass of whiskey slopping about but never quite spilling.

'One,' he counted on a finger. 'We know that there are several gates from this village into some sort of other world. Two. Long, long ago three people – a man, a girl and a boy came through the gates, following wyverns. And Jane Gwyer, who disappeared all those years ago, was probably one of them. Three. Somehow, we are descended from those people. Four. There's a key, and a book which will help us to open up the gates again and go through. And they will probably teach us how to call up the wyverns and use them, if we discover how.'

'Which do you want?' Thomas interrupted him.

Weever frowned.

Miss Aylmer sipped her punch.

'Five,' said Weever. 'We've lost our enemy. Parcel died in the fire at the Green Dragon, so we're clear to work together. We have to make the wyverns fly and open the gates again. Any gate will do.'

'Why?' Thomas demanded insistently.

Weever drained his glass and refilled it.

'Answer him, Clovis,' said Miss Aylmer.

'I've got an idea,' said Weever. 'Look.'

He gave Thomas a book.

'The church here,' said Weever. 'Saint Romanus. Look.'

Thomas read the page open before him.

' "Saint Romanus of Rouen. Bishop. About A.D. 639. Benedict, father of Saint Romanus, was of noble Frank family, related to Clovis. He was converted and baptised by Saint Remigius, probably at the same time as his royal master and kinsman. The wife of Benedict was Felicitas, and Romanus was their only son." – I don't understand,' said Thomas. 'What's all this about?'

Weever seized the book. 'Listen – "Saint Romanus is famed for his exploits in killing a great dragon, called Gargouille, which terrorised the city. He tracked it down to a dungeon and overcame it".'

He gave the book back to Thomas to look at.

Towser sniffed at Thomas's hands.

'Read the last bit,' said Weever. He was excited and poured himself another drink.

' "The feast day of Saint Romanus, October 23rd, was celebrated in Rouen with a procession, through the streets, of dragons made of combustible materials which were set alight at the end of the celebrations".'

'See?' said Weever.

'No,' said Thomas.

29

Weever snorted. 'Tell him, Felicity,' he said.

'Clovis,' she warned him. 'Be patient.'

'Answer my question,' said Thomas. 'What do you want to do? Do you want to go back? Or do you just want to have the wyverns to use however you want? Do you want to be a Dragon Master?'

'We'll have the procession this year,' said Weever. 'Here, with dragons and fireworks and everything.'

'No,' said Thomas.

'It will work,' said Weever. 'We'll call up the wyverns.'

'Or open the gates,' said Thomas. 'I won't do it. It's dangerous.'

'Not any more,' said Weever. 'Parcel's dead. There isn't an enemy any more.'

Thomas put his cup down and stood up. He looked tiny beside the huge man. 'There is,' he said. 'It's you. You're the enemy. You want the wyverns for yourself. I don't trust you.' He found himself shaking by the end of his speech.

'You fool,' said Weever. 'We have to work together.'

'No,' said Thomas. 'Ketches and Weevers don't get on. Remember?'

Weever looked as though he was about to strike Thomas when the sound of a wailing siren interrupted the confrontation.

'What's that?' said Felicity.

'Fire engine,' said Thomas.

They ran for the door together, but Thomas was first at the Green Dragon.

'What now?' Weever asked Felicity Aylmer.

'You made a mess of that,' she said. 'Let me have a try.'

The flames were high by the time the fire brigade arrived, and the crowd was growing.

'I don't understand,' said Bob Marl. 'This place should never have caught fire again.'

Harry was giving short, surly answers to the fire officer. Ted Ketch's answers were more detailed, but no more helpful. 'It just started. From nothing,' he explained.

'It's as though there's something deep down that's causing it,' said the fire officer. 'Something we can't reach.'

Harry gave him a hard look, then pointed to Weever. 'Ask him,' he said.

'I've just arrived,' said Weever cheerfully. 'I can't help, I'm afraid. Sorry.'

The crowd fell back, making a clear space around Weever, as though he had some contagious disease.

'But I'd like to be in touch with you during the week,' said Weever. 'To make arrangements for the 23rd. There'll be a bit of a fire risk that night.'

Then he turned his back and walked away from the restless crowd of villagers.

THREE

Mrs Reeves puffed out her fat cheeks and screwed up her piggy eyes in excitement.

'They're coming tonight,' she announced importantly.

Her pot leg was propped up on a stool, and she was sitting in her own armchair, pleased to be back home and the centre of attention.

Mrs Ketch looked at her curiously. She had popped in to offer some help, and had been surprised to find the room full of people, mostly new to the village.

Mrs Reeves did not seem to be very pleased to see Mrs Ketch, but she tried to hide it. And she was so excited about her news that she could not keep it to herself until Mrs Ketch had left.

There were murmurs of approval.

'Good thing, too.'

'I'm glad they're going to do something about him at last.'

'Are you sure, though?' asked Mrs Ketch.

Mrs Reeves bristled. 'I spoke to the man in charge,' she said. 'And he promised me that they would come this evening.'

'But the television people can't be interested in our Harvest Thanksgiving,' she argued.

'Not if we were having one,' said Mrs Reeves. 'That's just the point. But we're not.'

'Dog bites man,' Miss Snellgrove said, and looked as though she thought she had said something very wise. She was a very short woman, who strove, unsuccessfully, to look impressive.

'I don't follow you,' said Mrs Ketch.

'Village has Harvest Service. No story. No television.' Miss Snellgrove wagged her finger at Mrs Ketch. 'New vicar bans Harvest Service. Story. Television,' she said.

'Oh,' said Mrs Ketch. 'How very odd.'

Mrs Reeves felt that things were getting out of control and that she was losing her position as centre of attention. 'Not quite,' she corrected Miss Snellgrove. 'Villagers put on their own Harvest Service in opposition to the vicar. There's your story.'

'Tradition,' said Mrs Austin. 'We must keep up our traditions. There's always been a Harvest at Herpeton.'

'I'm not sure . . .' began Mrs Ketch.

Mrs Reeves seemed keen to change the subject. 'It's not just tradition,' she said.

'What, then?' asked Mrs Ketch.

'It's what's right,' snapped Mrs Reeves, feeling the authority seeping away from her.

'Why?' Mrs Ketch smiled as she asked the question.

'It's what we want,' said Mrs Austin.

'Ah,' said Mrs Ketch. 'That's not the same thing at all, but now I understand.'

Before a real argument could start the doorbell rang.

'Thank you for coming,' said Mrs Reeves. 'I'm sure you'll want to be getting along.'

'Oh, I'm fine,' said Mrs Ketch. 'I've got lots of time.' And she settled back in her chair as Mrs Reeves glared at her.

There was a sense of great expectancy while Mrs Austin answered the door, then a feeling of disappointment as a young woman was ushered in. Especially as the young woman was windswept, slim, and dressed in a loose, long skirt

34

and big shoes. Her hair was tied back with a silver clip.

Mrs Reeves frowned.

'This is Miss Thorpe,' said Mrs Austin.

'Nicky,' said the woman.

She looked around the room. No one spoke.

'Welcome,' said Mrs Ketch, to cover the embarrassing silence.

'Thanks.' Nicky grinned at her and put out her hand. 'I've just come to scout out the ground. See what's happening. Make a few contacts. You must be Mrs Reeves.'

'You're very young,' said Mrs Reeves, before Mrs Ketch could answer.

'Thank you,' said Nicky, who didn't sound grateful for the comment. 'Now, if we could just get . . .'

'Just a minute, young lady,' said Mrs Reeves.

Nicky's smile stayed on her face, but it was cold and set.

'Yes?'

'Where are the cameras?'

'Well, they'll come later, if we want to run the story.' She turned back to Mrs Ketch. 'If you could just let me have some background.' She took out notepad and a pencil.

'I'll tell you all there's to know,' said Mrs Reeves. 'This is my house. And it's my story.'

Nicky looked perplexed.

'Sorry,' said Mrs Ketch. 'The introductions

were a bit rushed. My name's Ketch. Barbara Ketch. That's Mrs Reeves.'

Mrs Reeves gave a smug smile as Nicky turned to her.

'Can you keep up?' she asked.

'I'll try.'

'I want you to get it all clear, so your boss knows it's a good story. We want lots of publicity.'

'Sorry?'

'I don't know why he didn't come himself in the first place. It would have been quicker.'

'I really don't know what you're talking about.'

'The one I spoke to on the phone. Mr Habgood. He should have come himself.'

'Oh. I see,' said Nicky. 'Jim. Well, he could have come, but he's too busy.'

'Huh!'

'He's got a lot of things to type up for me, and he couldn't have made the decision himself.'

'Oh?'

'He's my secretary. Now, shall we get the facts? You're all here because your vicar has axed your Harvest Service, and you want to put one on yourself in its place. Yes?' She scribbled as she spoke.

'Yes,' said Mrs Reeves.

'Tradition,' said Mrs Austin.

'No,' said Mrs Ketch.

All eyes turned to her.

'I'm just visiting the sick,' she said. 'I don't

36

want a Harvest.'

Nicky nodded enthusiastically and scribbled faster. 'Go on.'

'In fact I'll be helping the vicar with the Saint Romanus' Day celebrations. Lots of us will.'

'What's that?'

'Here,' said Mrs Reeves. 'What about our story?'

'It's traditional here,' said Mrs Ketch. 'It goes back hundreds of years. Dragons and fireworks and . . .'

'That's enough,' snapped Mrs Reeves.

'Yes, I think it is,' said Mrs Ketch. She stood up. 'I think I'd better go. I hope you get better soon,' she said to Mrs Reeves.

'But . . .' said Nicky.

'I'll show you out,' said Miss Snellgrove.

'I can find my own way.'

'But your story,' said Nicky.

'My story,' said Mrs Reeves.

'I live across the green,' said Mrs Ketch. 'I'll be there.'

'Give me ten minutes,' said Nicky.

'Now just a minute,' Mrs Reeves complained.

'Fifteen at the most,' said Nicky.

'See you.'

Mrs Ketch closed the door on a chaos of complaint and she smiled.

It was over a week since Thomas had refused to

have anything to do with the Saint Romanus celebrations, and he and Weever hadn't spoken since.

Felicity Aylmer took her courage in both hands when she knocked on his door to try to persuade him to help.

Towser yelped with pleasure when he saw her, and Thomas had to admit to himself that there was something about her that he liked, despite her friendship with Weever. But he couldn't think what it was.

'I hope you're not going to keep me on the doorstep,' she said.

'Sorry. Come in. Mum's out, though.'

'That's a pity,' said Miss Aylmer, who had watched Mrs Ketch leave and had been waiting for a chance to speak to Thomas alone. 'I don't mind waiting.'

The wait was a silent one at first. It made Thomas feel uncomfortable, so he said the first thing that came into his head.

'You look like Jane Gwyer.'

'Excuse me?'

'Nothing.'

'Do I?' she asked.

'Yes.'

'I'd never noticed.'

'Forget it.'

The silence closed around them again.

Towser jumped on to Miss Aylmer's lap, where

she fondled him. And although Thomas frowned Towser stayed there quite cheerfully.

'You nearly got lost, didn't you?' said Felicity.

Thomas was cross with himself for giving in, but he couldn't stop himself asking, 'When did I? What do you mean?'

'Not you,' she said. 'Towser. When Parcel captured him and locked him in the Manor.'

'What was he doing there?' asked Thomas. 'Making experiments on those animals.'

'I think it's all linked with Jane Gwyer,' said Felicity. 'The legend is that she was wonderful with animals. I think that he had a confused idea that if he filled her house with animals and did nasty things to them, she might come back, and he'd capture her. Or,' she paused, 'perhaps he thought that there was some power round here, and that if he experimented with the animals he would discover the secrets of the wyverns. He was a bad man, and not very clear in his head.'

'Is that it?' said Thomas. 'It sounds stupid.'

'But it just might have worked. Who knows? Stranger things have been going on here lately.'

The wind rattled the door, and pushed a dead leaf underneath it.

'Why?' asked Thomas.

'Hmm?'

'Why have strange things been going on? My dad never saw a wyvern. And he says there haven't been any for hundreds of years. And he's a Ketch.'

'I think things are coming to an end here,' said Felicity. 'I'm not sure why. But it's finishing.'

'Why?' Thomas asked again.

Felicity hesitated. 'You won't like the answer,' she warned him.

'Go on, though,' he said.

'There have always been Ketches here. That hasn't changed, but there hasn't been a Gwyer since 1781, when Jane Gwyer disappeared. I think she ran away from something.'

'Parcel?'

'Probably.'

'Where to?'

'America, I think. Massachusetts.'

'That's where you come from.'

'Yes. Where the witches were.'

'Oh.' Thomas took some time to take this in.

'And there hasn't been a Weever here for even longer,' she said.

'When?'

'There was a Weever who tried to destroy the old stone circle. One of the gates.'

'Stonekiller Weever,' said Thomas. 'The man who tried to smash the stone circle hundreds of years ago.'

'Yes. He must have been trying to close the gate for ever; to destroy it for some reason. He must have been going mad.'

Thomas could picture a huge, dark man, with

mad eyes, hammering the stones to splinters, trying desperately to open the gate.

'No,' he said. 'He was trying to go home.'

Felicity looked at him carefully. 'I guess you know best.'

'He's bad,' said Thomas. 'Like Parcel.'

'He's dangerous,' said Felicity. 'That's not the same thing. And I guess he's desperate.'

'I won't help him,' said Thomas. 'I won't.'

Felicity sighed.

'What does he want, anyway?' the boy said, his freckled nose crinkling in thought. 'What will he do if we can open a gate, or make the wyverns fly?'

'What are you frightened of?'

'I'm not frightened, but you said yourself, he's dangerous. He wants all the power for himself. Doesn't he?' Thomas stared at her, demanding an answer.

The door banged open, caught by the strong wind, and Mrs Ketch hurried in.

'Brr! That's sharp, that wind,' she said. 'Oh, hello! Is Thomas looking after you?'

'I'll go upstairs,' said Thomas. He stood up.

Miss Aylmer gritted her teeth in frustration.

'We're going to be on television,' said Mrs Ketch.

'What?' Miss Aylmer looked horrified.

'Why?' asked Thomas.

'That stupid Mrs Reeves told them about the

Harvest being cancelled.'

'They won't be interested in that,' said Felicity.

'Local news,' said Mrs Ketch. 'They'll show anything.'

'Will there have to be a Harvest?' asked Felicity.

'Do you think Weever will give in?' said Mrs Ketch. She did not need an answer.

'Especially if he's being threatened by the television people,' said Felicity. 'He'll really dig his heels in.'

'I'm going to help him,' said Mrs Ketch.

'What?' Thomas demanded.

'With the Saint Romanus celebrations.'

'You can't!' he shouted.

'You just watch me. He'll need some help.'

'You're not a Ketch!' He yelled. 'You don't belong.'

'Thomas,' said Felicity.

'Neither do you!' he shouted. He raised his arm and pushed back his sandy hair from over his eyes.

'Go upstairs!' Mrs Ketch ordered him. 'Right now!'

'Oh, but I do,' said Felicity. 'And so does Weever. We all three belong.' She pointed to his arm where the sleeve had fallen away. The purple mark was deeper now, longer. Pushing back her own sleeve, she showed Thomas a similar mark, only more distinct, like a tattoo shaped like a

42

dragon. 'And we're all three here. For the first time in hundreds of years, there's a Ketch, a Weever and a Gwyer, all together in Herpeton. What are you going to do about it?'

Thomas looked helpless. 'Leave me alone!' he shouted, louder than ever.

A low voice came from the doorway.

'Sorry,' said Nicky Thorpe. 'Am I interrupting? I knocked, but there was no answer. I'll come back later, if you'd rather.'

FOUR

Every television in Herpeton was tuned in for the local news.

Mrs Reeves sat impatiently while the newsreader went through stories of traffic accidents and factories closing and the local MP protesting about something to do with Europe. Then, she sat forward in her chair when she heard the words:

'... and finally, we go over to the sleepy village

of Herpeton, where a war is about to start between the vicar and his parishioners. Nicky Thorpe reports.'

The screen, and all the other screens in the village, showed a windswept Nicky Thorpe, standing in front of the statue of Jane Gwyer on the village green. She was holding a microphone in one hand and cradling a huge vegetable marrow with her other arm.

'You wouldn't think that there was much to get worked up about in a quiet village like Herpeton. But you'd be wrong. Some of the villagers are furious that there will be no Harvest Thanksgiving this year.' The screen blinked and Mrs Reeves's face appeared. In her house; the real Mrs Reeves smiled.

'It's just like you,' said Miss Snellgrove.

'Hush! It is me. It's film,' said Mrs Reeves.

'It's the new vicar,' said the Mrs Reeves on the television. 'He doesn't understand our ways. But we won't give in. We'll have our Harvest.'

Nicky's face reappeared. 'But that's not the end of the story,' she said.

'I said lots more than that,' Mrs Reeves protested. 'They interviewed me for ages.'

Miss Snellgrove shushed her. 'We're missing the vicar.'

'What?' Mrs Reeves yelped. 'What's he doing there?'

'So you see,' said Weever. 'Harvest is a very

new service. We're going back to the old ways.'

'Humph,' snorted Mrs Reeves.

'Tell me a little about it,' Nicky encouraged him.

'There'll be a big procession, with a dragon, made of paper, with people inside it. And a bonfire. And kites. And fireworks. All just as it has been for centuries. The way it used to be here in Herpeton.'

'So,' said Nicky, turning back to the camera. 'The battle lines are drawn up, and the war is about to begin. The vicar, on the side of the old ways, and some of the villagers wanting what they've become used to. Tell me,' she said to Weever. 'Do you have any support for your plans?'

'No!' rapped Mrs Reeves to the screen.

'Oh yes,' said Weever, as though he could hear her and was answering her. 'There's Harry, for instance.'

Harry Dobbs blinked at the camera.

'That old fool,' said Miss Snellgrove.

'I'd like to see the wyverns fly,' said Harry.

'Wyverns?' asked Nicky.

'That's what we calls dragons in Herpeton.'

'And I'll be helping to make the dancing dragon,' said Miss Aylmer.

'And I'll be giving a mind to the songs,' said Ted Ketch.

'Traitors,' said Mrs Reeves.

The screen blinked again, and her piggy eyes

gleamed out at them.

'Do you have much support for your scheme?' Nicky asked.

'The whole village is with me,' Mrs Reeves assured her.

'She cheated me!' said Mrs Reeves. 'She's made a fool of me!'

She grabbed the remote control and flicked the television off.

'So,' said Nicky, back live on camera in other homes. 'There'll be fireworks in Herpeton one way or another. We'll keep an eye on events for you, and we'll let . . .'

She did not finish her sentence because Weever pushed her out of camera and sent her sprawling to the muddy ground.

Thomas had been enjoying the show.

He had also been enjoying making Weever angry. He knew that the man really needed his help to call up the wyverns, and Thomas was determined not to give it to him. But he was unhappy that he had no one to talk to about things.

'And you shouldn't have anything to do with him, either,' he told his mother.

'I'm not going to argue with you,' Mrs Ketch smiled.

His father was, surprisingly, no better.

'You're a Ketch,' Thomas badgered him. 'You shouldn't be working with Weever. Weevers and

Ketches don't mix.'

They were standing outside their cottage, looking at the green and the activity taking place with the television crew.

Ted Ketch kept as good humoured with Thomas as his wife, but no more helpful.

'I've never known a Weever before,' he told Thomas. 'So I don't know about not mixing. But I want to help to do anything I can to make the wyverns fly. So I'm with him.'

'But he'll steal the wyverns from us,' Thomas insisted. 'Don't you see?'

Ted thought about this.

'I don't see as how he can,' he said. 'Seeing as how they aren't ours to steal.'

'But they could be,' Thomas persisted. 'I've made them fly again.' He huddled into his coat, against the keen wind.

'Have you?'

'I've seen them. So have you.'

'That's true enough,' Ted admitted. 'I've seen them. But I don't know that you made them fly, did you?'

'Of course I did.'

'All right, then. Make them fly now.'

Thomas ground his teeth in exasperation. 'I don't know how to!'

'Then how do you know you did before?'

'I just know.'

Ted put his arm round Thomas. 'I'm sorry,' he

said. 'Perhaps you're right. Perhaps you did make them fly. But unless you know how to do it again, it's not much good, is it? You haven't got an idea. You haven't got a plan. But Weever has. And I think we should help him with it.'

He looked kindly at Thomas and waited for him to answer.

So many thoughts were fighting inside Thomas's head that he couldn't think where to start.

'He doesn't belong here,' he said at last.

'Well now, if what they say is right, then neither do I. Neither do you.'

Thomas frowned. His sandy fringe fell over his eyes.

'Do you want to go back?' he asked.

Ted looked at him. 'Where to?'

'Through the gate. Back to where the wyverns came from.'

'No,' said Ted. 'No, I don't.'

'Why not?'

'Well, for a start, I don't feel as though I want to. I feel I belong here. And for another thing, I might get through, because I'm a Ketch. And so might you. But I doubt your mother would. She's not a Ketch. She just married one. And I wouldn't go anywhere without her.'

'No,' agreed Thomas.

'But what about you? Do you want to go back?'

Weever raised a huge arm and waved to Ted

and Thomas. Ted waved back. Thomas growled. 'Ignore him,' he said.

'I can't do that.'

'You can.'

'But I don't want to.'

'I can't talk to you any more,' said Thomas. 'Not if you're going to help him.'

And he sped off before his father could say anything more. He skirted the green, avoiding the television crew's thick cables that stretched out like sleeping snakes, and he found himself a sheltered spot, by the stone wall of the grave-yard. At first the thoughts of his conversation with his father tumbled through his mind, keeping him tense and angry, but, as time went on, he became involved in what was happening on the green, and he forgot.

'You want to be on television?' asked a cheerful voice.

'No.'

'Can't say I blame you. Lot of standing around in the cold.'

'Yes.'

'Don't say much, do you?'

'No,' said Thomas, who didn't want to be rude, but couldn't think of anything else he could say.

The man laughed.

Thomas felt relieved and laughed with him.

'Henry,' said the man. 'What's your name?'

'Thomas.'

'Couldn't take hold of this, could you?'

Thomas took a bag of screwdrivers from Henry, who tinkered, unconvincingly, with a junction box. Thomas could not keep his eyes from Henry's arms. His sleeves were rolled up, and the forearms were thick and knotted with muscles. Every inch of them was covered with swirling tattoos.

'She came to our house,' said Thomas.

'Nicky?'

'Yes. I didn't like her.'

'She's all right. I've worked with worse.'

'She wants Weever to play tricks,' said Thomas.

'The big bloke? The vicar?'

'Yes.'

'What sort of tricks?' said Henry.

Thomas hesitated.

Henry waited.

'Stupid tricks,' said Thomas. 'He thinks he can conjure up dragons.'

Henry whistled.

'That's a good trick,' he said. 'If he can do it.'

'He can't,' said Thomas, who was feeling very guilty about talking in that way about the wyverns.

'That's the nearest he'll get, I reckon,' said Henry. He looked up and Thomas followed the line of his eyes. Perched on a gleaming golden ball on the pinnacle of the steeple was a bronze wyvern, its wings spread out, its mouth gaping against the wind.

'I'll have a word with Nicky,' said Henry. 'Make sure she gets a shot of that.'

'Why?'

'Good background,' said Henry. 'We could even shoot a scene from up there.'

Thomas felt his head swim and his eyes blur as he looked up and imagined being perched there with the dragon.

'You couldn't get up there,' he said.

'There's steps,' said Henry. 'See?'

He pointed.

'No,' said Thomas.

'Set into the tiles of the steeple. Like handholds and footrests.'

Thomas squinted, and thought he might be able to see them. But he wasn't sure.

'Must be there so they can clean the weather vane,' he said.

'Or fix it, more like,' said Henry. 'Temperamental things.'

'Weather vanes?' asked Thomas.

'Dragons,' said Henry.

Thomas stared at him, in case the man was making fun of him, but Henry looked serious enough.

'I'd better get on,' he said. 'They'll be going out soon.'

'Going out?'

'Broadcasting. See you.'

Thomas felt lonely when Henry had left, in a way he hadn't before. He cheered up when Nicky started organising Harry and Weever, and getting them ready to speak to the camera. He scowled when his father was included. But he had a good time watching, and thinking that he was the most important person in Herpeton, the one they should be talking to. And he felt a sort of satisfaction that he wouldn't take part; satisfied until Weever picked up his black skirts, pushed the small crowd aside, lunged forward and flung himself at Nicky in a rugby tackle that sent her flying to the ground several yards from where she had been standing.

There was instant uproar.

Thomas leaped to his feet. Towser ran round in circles, yapping. The cameraman, as cameramen always do, offered no help, but tried to keep his camera fixed firmly on Nicky, as she sprawled beneath Weever.

Then, with a sigh, the heavy statue of Jane Gwyer toppled over and smashed to the ground, landing exactly where Nicky had been standing.

FIVE

Harry Dobbs looked at the fallen statue and shook his head. 'There'll be more trouble,' he said. 'I said there would. You mark what I say, someone's going to get killed before this is all over.'

Thomas shuddered, and the words would not go out of his head.

The lively, jokey atmosphere had disappeared, and the crowd was uneasy, disturbed.

Mrs Ketch bent over Nicky.

Weever heaved his great bulk back to its feet.

The camera kept filming.

The wind whipped round them, suddenly more fierce, more penetrating.

Ted Ketch helped Nicky to sit up. She was shaking and white.

Thomas elbowed his way through the crowd, trying to get near, to see what was happening.

Miss Aylmer stood aside a little, to allow him some space.

Nicky was trying to speak into her microphone and keep the broadcast going, but she was stammering and not making much sense.

'We'll go home and have some tea,' said Mrs Ketch.

'So, there's more excitement in Herpeton,' said Nicky.

'That'll do,' said Mrs Ketch. She took the microphone away from her and gave it to Henry, who was the nearest person who looked as though he knew what he was doing.

'Give her lots of sugar,' he said.

'I've got to carry on,' said Nicky.

'You're coming home,' said Mrs Ketch, leading her away. She turned to the cameraman. 'And you can put that thing away,' she said. 'You're not coming with me.'

'Got to,' said the cameraman. And he tried to follow, but Mrs Ketch shut her door firmly in his face.

'He could have killed her,' said Thomas.

'He saved her life, I think,' said Miss Aylmer.

Weever was brushing his cassock, pointlessly, for the mud was wet, and he only succeeded in spreading it even more and making things worse. He walked round and round the fallen statue.

'Can't be the wind,' he said, though the wind was very fierce now, and was whipping the wyvern weather vane round and screaming as it rushed through its open mouth.

Jane Gwyer's blind eyes stared down at the muddy ground. For over a hundred years she had looked out over the changing fields, watching the seasons flow. Now she regarded the earth beneath her.

Towser sniffed round by the base of the plinth, and started to burrow down, his claws scratching against the stone, but making good headway underneath.

One moment he was digging away, the next he had gone.

Thomas yelled.

'Towser!'

'What's up?' asked Henry.

'He's gone.'

Thomas was wild-eyed with panic.

'That dog's always in trouble,' said Weever.

'You shut up!' shouted Thomas. 'You just shut up!'

Miss Aylmer put her fingers in her mouth

and whistled.

Towser's head poked out of the hole beneath the plinth and he grinned at them with his pink tongue sticking out of his mouth. He clawed furiously with his front legs, and was out again. Thomas grabbed his collar and held him tight.

'Looks like subsidence,' said Henry. 'Under the base.'

Weever nodded. 'The ground's not very safe round here,' he agreed. 'There are old tunnels everywhere.'

'Better rope it off,' said Henry.

'What are you going to do about all this, Weever?' asked Harry Dobbs.

'All what?'

'These accidents. Mrs Reeves. The fire at the pub and now this. Something's happening.'

'Coincidences,' said Weever.

'There'll be more before we're finished,' said Harry.

'What if there are? What can I do?' Weever asked.

'You're the cause of it,' said Harry.

'Am I?'

'I reckon so.'

Weever looked at Thomas. 'It might be someone else,' he said.

Thomas scowled.

Harry thought about it. 'You might be right at that,' he agreed.

'Are you still going to help?' asked Weever.

'With the St Romanus' Day?' said Harry.

'Yes.'

'Wouldn't miss it for owt,' said Harry.

'But it's causing all this trouble,' said Thomas. 'You can't. How can you?'

'Reckon it's got to be done sooner or later,' said Harry. 'I've a mind to be around when it's done, and see what happens.'

The group of villagers, who had been standing around listening to this exchange, moved silently away.

Thomas pulled at Towser and made towards his cottage.

'Will you help?' Harry called after him. 'I reckon you'd be useful.'

'No!' shouted Thomas. 'Not for anyone.'

And for the next few days he felt a stranger in his own village.

There was a fury of activity.

Mrs Reeves sat in her house, with her pot leg propped up, surrounded by a band of helpers and piles of paper.

GREAT HARVEST FESTIVAL SERVICE
SUNDAY OCTOBER 25TH
IN SAINT ROMANUS' CHURCH
HERPETON
3.00 PM.

'He'll have to let us in,' she predicted. 'He won't dare stop us.'

'But who will take the service?' asked Miss Snellgrove.

Mrs Reeves had not yet worked this out in her own mind. On the one hand, she wanted to force Weever to take it. On the other hand, she did not want him to have any part in it.

Mrs Austin picked up one of the handbills. 'We can't put these through people's doors,' she said. 'Not without his permission.'

'Don't be so timid,' snapped Mrs Reeves.

'But he could lock us out. There'd be all those people standing outside, with their arms full of vegetables,' she said.

'He wouldn't dare!' Mrs Reeves said.

'He is the vicar,' said Mrs Austin.

'Not for much longer. Not if I've got anything to do with it,' Mrs Reeves said.

'Ooh,' said Miss Snellgrove. 'What do you mean?'

'Wait and see,' she said, darkly. 'Wait and see. Now, off you go, and put one of these through every door in the village.'

Miss Snellgrove gathered up an armful, but Mrs Austin hesitated. 'I'll do mine tomorrow,' she promised. 'I've just got to pop home for a minute.'

'She'll never do it,' said Mrs Reeves, as Mrs Austin disappeared. 'Too timid!'

'Well,' said Miss Snellgrove.

'But I know I can depend on you,' said Mrs Reeves.

Miss Snellgrove, whose desire to be liked was stronger than her fear of Weever, smiled back and scuttled off.

In the new vicarage, the kites were taking shape, and the loops of wire and swathes of crêpe and tissue paper were being arranged for the dancing dragon.

Weever had brought in children from the surrounding villages because Herpeton had no school any more and Thomas was the only boy left living there.

Harry Dobbs had taken charge of the dancing dragon, and was determined to be the head.

'I don't care who follows behind,' he said. 'But I'm going to lead.'

'There'll be six more of you inside it,' said Weever, who was looming over the activity.

'Or seven,' said Felicity, 'depending on how long the tail is. I'm having some trouble looping the last section of wire, and I can't cut it or I'll leave a dangerous point.'

'What if we all go in different directions?' asked Harry. 'We'll tear this stuff. It's right flimsy.'

'You'll be tied together with webbing, so you won't be able to wander off,' said Weever. 'Everything's under control.'

'Is that right?' said Harry. 'Under control is it?'

The cameraman moved around, filming the industry, catching the colours of the paper and ribbons, the textures of the materials, the intricate looping of the wire.

Nicky was talking quietly to people, taking her time, getting down on the floor with them, getting her fingers sticky with glue, getting her face smudged with paint, until they quite forgot that she was there to ask them questions, and they talked quite naturally, as though their voices were not being recorded on her tape.

The wind buffeted the windows and made the chimney whine.

'So, everything's going ahead?' she asked Weever.

'Looks like it.'

'Not quite,' said Felicity.

'What's missing?' asked Nicky.

'The Wyvern Songs,' said Felicity.

'They'll be sung,' said Weever.

'Ah, but who by?' asked Felicity.

There was silence.

'Do you know?' asked Nicky.

'By me,' said Weever. 'And by the children. I'm getting them the words.'

'Fat lot of good that will do,' said Felicity.

Nicky left her tape recorder running, but she said nothing. She had often found that was the best way to get what she wanted, and she could always edit the tape later.

'It's the songs that matter,' said Weever. 'Not the singer.'

Felicity made a cross sound with her mouth.

'You'll get nowhere without Thomas Ketch,' she said. 'And you know it.'

Nicky interrupted, despite her plan to keep quiet. 'Who's Thomas Ketch?'

'Ssh,' said Weever.

Nicky looked startled.

Felicity nodded across to a group of women who were stitching tails for kites, and red ribbons for the flames from the wyverns' mouths. Weever raised a finger to his lips.

Nicky pushed her hair out of her eyes and looked. She recognised Mrs Ketch, but remembered only that her name was Barbara. The other women were strangers to her. But she had guessed enough to realise that she would learn more by keeping quiet for a while. She quickly scribbled 'Thomas Kitch' in her notebook and gave it to Weever. He struck out the 'i' and put in an 'e', so that it read 'Thomas Ketch'. Nicky nodded her thanks and tucked the notebook away.

'Have I met him?' she asked.

'I doubt it,' said Weever. 'He's been keeping out of the way.'

Harry Dobbs's head poked out from under the dragon. 'He's old Herpeton, like us,' he said.

'I didn't see you there, Harry,' said Weever.

'I thought maybe you'd not,' said Harry, and he disappeared into the head again, to fix the jaw bones of the mouth so that it would open and shut.

Felicity gave Nicky a warning look.

Harry's head popped out again. 'But you'll get nowt for all this carry on if you don't get Ketch to sing,' he warned. 'I'll tell you that.' And he was gone again.

'Talk to you later,' said Nicky. 'I'm going for some fresh air.'

'Wrap up warm, then,' said Felicity.

'I'll come with you,' Weever offered.

'No. I'll need some time to think about things,' said Nicky.

Weever scowled. 'Suit yourself.'

Thomas walked round the circle of monoliths that made up Parcel's Stones. He was careful not to let his foot go over the boundary and into the circle itself. Towser, perfectly happy, ran in and out, pink tongue lolling out and steam rising from his mouth in the chill, autumn afternoon air.

Thomas watched him uneasily.

'Come on, Towser. Don't go in there,' he called.

So Towser ran straight through the centre of the stones and out again, then recrossed and ended up next to Thomas, who sighed and decided to give up and let him run where he wanted. But still Thomas was careful not to go in there himself.

He found a place sheltered from the wind, sat down, with his back resting against the tall stone, and opened up a bag he had carried on his back. The ground sloped away from the circle, it was not too soft or muddy.

He looked around, then he took an old leather bound book from the bag. He rested the book on his knees, looked in the bag again, and drew out a large iron key. Thomas held the key, turning it over and over in his hands, enjoying the feel of the cold metal, the weight, and the rounded handle. Then he took out a green glass bottle, with a raised wyvern embossed in the glass. He smoothed his hands over this and stroked it. He took out the stopper and sniffed at the neck, though it was empty.

He rested all three objects on his legs, keeping his hands on them, leaned back against the stone and looked around.

The pasture where the circle was set fell away and met an ancient hedgerow. Beyond the bushes a tractor trundled over the field, dragging its plough and cutting into the earth.

The blades sliced through the green ground, lifted it, turned it, and let the sillion slide back down, with smooth shining edge.

Thomas could hear the rattling of the engine, but not the scrape of the plough.

He saw black shapes circle round behind the plough, then swoop and dive, to search the new-turned earth for worms. They looked huge and ungainly against the low sun, like dragons in flight, but Thomas knew they were only rooks.

He opened the book, turned the pages carefully, frowning at the strange script and the mysterious drawings.

Stopping at a page he examined it carefully, looking closely at the pattern the words made on the page, even though he could not read them.

Putting his finger on the words he began to sing, softly:

> 'Wyvern Weever
> Wyvern Weever
> Weever wyvern
> Threw the stones.
>
> Fly, wyvern, fly
> Through the night.
> Darken the sky
> With deadly flight.
>
> Wyvern Weever
> Wyvern Weever
> Weever wyvern
> Threw the stones.

Sail, wyvern, sail,
Through the sky.
Flourish your tail
As clouds go by.

Wyvern Weever
Wyvern Weever
Weever wyvern
Threw the stones.

Die, wyvern, die.
For ages long
Wait for the cry
Of wyvern song.

Wyvern Weever
Wyvern Weever
Weever wyvern
Threw the stones.

Burn, wyvern, burn
In the deep earth's heart.
Turn, wyvern, turn
When dangers start.

Wyvern Weever
Wyvern Weever
Weever wyvern
Threw the stones.

> Wyvern, return
> Through ages long,
> When we learn
> The wyvern song.
>
> Wyvern Weever
> Wyvern Weever
> Weever wyvern
> Threw the stones.

That's it, Towser!' he shouted. 'That's it!'

Towser trotted over, wagged his tail, agreeably, sat down and grinned up at Thomas.

'Look,' said Thomas. 'The lines are just the same, and there are the same number of words. It's the Weever Song, in that strange language. Listen.'

And Thomas sang again, for Towser, tracing his finger on the words as he did. He was just over halfway through when he noticed that Towser was no longer looking at him, but was looking up, over Thomas's left shoulder. Thomas turned his head and saw Nicky.

'What are you doing here?' he demanded, rudely. 'Spying on me.'

SIX

'I'm sorry,' said Nicky. 'I didn't mean to frighten you.'

'You didn't,' said Thomas, annoyed to think that she might believe he was afraid. 'You took me by surprise. You sneaked up on me.'

'No,' said Nicky. 'I just walked up. I didn't know you were here at first.'

'Then why did you come?'

'I wanted to be on my own. To think about

68

something.'

Towser snuffled his nose against the back of her hand. She pushed her hair out of her eyes, smiled and stroked him.

'What have you got there?' she asked Thomas.

Thomas pushed the book and the bottle into the bag, and put the key in his pocket. He did not answer her.

'Mind if I sit down?'

Nicky did not wait for an answer, but slid down next to him, her back also against the broad, tall stone.

Thomas knew he could not stop her, and he did not want to walk off, but he made up his mind not to talk to her.

'It was creepy, walking through the circle,' she said.

This was the one thing that Thomas needed to know about, so he lost his silence.

'Why?' he asked.

'It made me feel dizzy.'

'Sick?'

'No. Just sort of unsteady. Like I was really high up.'

'I hate heights,' said Thomas.

'So do I.' Nicky smiled at him, and, despite his hostility to her, he smiled back.

'I need some help,' said Nicky.

'I can't help.'

'You don't know what it is yet. Look at those

birds following the plough. I wish I had a crew here.'

'Crew?' asked Thomas.

'Camera. There's so much I want to film, so much I need to know. That's the trouble with this village.'

'What?'

'No one tells me everything. They only tell me their own little bits. I can't fit all the pieces together.'

'It's not that hard,' said Thomas.

'I think so.'

They sat for a long time in silence. The sun sank quickly, and the air grew colder. The tractor wove up and down the field, turning the earth.

'That looks violent,' said Nicky.

'What?'

'Like it must hurt the land to be torn like that.'

Thomas had never thought of it like that before.

'It's used to it,' he said. 'It doesn't hurt.'

'You never get used to some things,' said Nicky. 'Not if they hurt a lot.'

Thomas picked at a loose thread at the neck of his bag, embarrassed.

'I used to wish that bad things wouldn't happen,' said Nicky. 'And they never did. I was lucky.'

'I wished like that,' Thomas said.

'Then, one day, I made the biggest wish ever.'

There was another long silence. The tractor lifted the bright blades of the sharp plough and left the field.

'My mum was in a car crash,' said Nicky. 'And I got to the hospital where she was, and I wished so hard that she would be all right. I sat there all night, wishing.'

Towser licked her hand.

The sun dipped behind a spinney and the evening light turned to dusk.

Nicky stood up.

'I'd better get back,' she said. 'We'll have to pay the crew overtime if we finish after 5 o'clock.'

Thomas watched her stand.

'Coming?' she asked.

'All right.'

Thomas led Nicky round the circle.

'It's quicker to go through the middle,' she said.

'What was it you wanted to know about the village?' he asked.

'Why are they fighting? It isn't really about the Harvest Service, is it?'

'No.'

'And who are the old village, and who are the new people? And why don't they get on?'

Thomas explained who everyone was, and then he found himself telling her about the wyverns, and the girl, Franny, who had gone through to the other world, and how Weever and Felicity Aylmer belonged through the gate in that other world.

They reached the village long before the story was over, and they leaned against the churchyard wall while Thomas explained. He took out the key and the bottle and the book and he showed her them.

Nicky was very excited when she saw the book.

'Can I film it? Please?'

He shook his head.

'It's really secret. I shouldn't even show you.'

She squeezed his arm. 'Thank you. I'm glad you did.'

There was another silence between them. Thomas knew he still hadn't told her anything about himself, nor about how he came to have the things, nor that he, too, was descended from a person who had come through the gate, from the wyvern world.

'There's something else,' said Nicky.

'Oh?'

'I need to meet someone, but I think he's avoiding me.'

'Who?' Thomas pushed the things away, quickly, trying to hide them, wishing that the dusk and the walk home had not made him trust her.

'An old man.'

Thomas relaxed.

'Harry Dobbs. I told you about him.'

'No. I know Harry.'

72

'Who?'

'Thomas Ketch.'

'What?'

'He's a singer.'

'Why do you want him?'

'To sing the Wyvern Songs. They say he's got the secret of the wyverns, so we really need him for the programme.'

Thomas backed away.

'You cheated me,' he said. 'You're a spy.'

He ran off, calling to Towser to follow him.

Towser gave Nicky a last snuffle, then bounded off after Thomas.

'Oh, damn,' said Nicky. She walked along the edge of the wall, towards the new vicarage. 'I blew that. But how? What did I do wrong?'

'What?' said Weever, stepping from the porch of the church.

'That boy,' said Nicky. Thomas ran past the statue of Jane Gwyer, still fallen on the wet earth. 'He was telling me all sorts of things, then he ran off.'

'Thomas Ketch,' said Weever.

'Him? He can't be. Thomas Ketch is old. Harry said so.'

'Old Herpeton,' said Weever. 'Not an old person.'

'Damn,' said Nicky again. Then she remembered how she had wanted to tell him about her mother. 'But old as well,' she said.

The church clock struck.

'What's that?' asked Nicky.

'Quarter past.'

'Oh, no.'

'What?'

'Now I'm really in trouble. We'll have to pay the crew overtime.'

'Send them home, then come round to the old vicarage for a drink. Bring Felicity,' said Weever. 'I'll light a fire.'

'Not today,' said Nicky. 'But listen, why doesn't he want to help to raise the wyverns?'

'Thomas Ketch?'

'Yes.'

'You must ask him that.'

'I'll try,' said Nicky. 'But I think he won't talk to me again.'

Thomas didn't talk to anyone for a while – not about anything important. He kept his distance from the camera now, and the technicians, and the Harvest Service people, and the Saint Romanus' celebration people. And he especially kept away from Nicky Thorpe.

She tried to catch him, once.

'Thomas!' she called, as she saw him run across the green. 'Look at this!'

But Thomas darted off, round the churchyard wall and off across the fields towards the stone circle. He hated the circle. It made him shudder to be near it. But he was drawn there again and again, against his will. He sat with his back to the stone he had leaned against the day he talked to Nicky. And it felt warm under him, and he felt as though it was pulling him towards it.

He had a plan.

He was making a kite of his own. In the book, Thomas Kych's book, that the girl had brought from the wyvern world, there was a picture of a man flying a kite. Thomas copied that kite.

It was difficult, especially as he was keeping it a secret.

The wyvern's body was long and curved. It had wings as well as legs. This was the problem. Thomas made a first model, half the size he intended to use, and he made it with tissue paper and cane. The wind grabbed it greedily and ripped the wings clean off.

Thomas puzzled about what to do.

He tried crépe paper instead, and he made the struts out of plastic straws instead of light cane. The straws were more flexible, and took the wind better, bending just enough to make the wings fly, rather than snap. The crépe paper howled against the wind, but it held.

'Brilliant,' said Thomas. 'Brilliant.'

The wyvern dipped and bobbed, and flew with its wings stretched and mouth wide. It did not soar, and was dangerously close to the ground several times. The string was thin, but still too heavy. It was dragging the kite down. He was using garden twine – thin and strong, and fairly light, but still too heavy to allow the kite to rise up.

As he pulled the kite against the wind, Thomas saw someone walking in his direction, so he reeled the wyvern in on its string, and examined it quickly. One leg had twisted out of shape and was beginning to shear off from the body, but Thomas reckoned he could improve that on the larger model. And he hadn't used the ribbons for the flames from the mouth, but they wouldn't add enough extra weight to make it a problem. He looked up and saw that the figure was approaching him, so he dismantled the kite and put the pieces carefully into his bag. When Harry Dobbs drew near, Thomas was leaning against his stone and trying to look as though he was doing nothing. He was glad he had hidden the kite in time.

'Fair old wind,' said Harry.

'Yes.'

'Couldn't hardly hear yourself sing in this,' he said.

'I wasn't singing,' said Thomas.

'They are down there,' said Harry.

'Oh.'

'Fit to bust,' he added.

Thomas picked up his bag and looked ready to leave. 'Singing about ploughing and planting,' he said. 'Harvest. So what?'

Harry scratched his neck. 'No, not ploughing.'

Thomas walked away.

'Something about a wyvern on a steeple,' said Harry.

'What?'

'She's making a film of 'em, singing away.'

'Who?'

'That television woman.'

Thomas was white with anger. 'No! Who is? Who's singing?'

'All of 'em. Not me. I can't sing.' He proved this by opening his mouth and croaking:

> 'Riding the clouds on a pointed perch
> The wyvern runs to the east.'

He carried on singing tunelessly as Thomas sped away from him, his sandy hair streaming out behind him, his legs racing across the grass, his eyes watering with the sting of the cold wind in his face. The bag thumped against his back. Towser's little legs flashed in his effort to keep up with Thomas.

The group of children was gathered round the porch of the church. The camera was pointing to the wyvern weather vane, which gleamed in the cold sun and moved very slightly as the wind buffeted it.

Weever was keeping them to time. Ted Ketch,

Thomas's father, was mouthing the words to them, to make sure they did not stumble.

'She lifts her nose to scent the breeze
That brings sweet rest from the south.
The wyvern's wings sweep back with ease,
As she stretches up with laughing mouth
To ride the wind.'

'Shut up!' shouted Thomas, scattering the small choir.

Weever stopped, his arms in mid-air, still conducting.

Ted strode forward and grabbed Thomas.

'What do you think you're doing?' he demanded.

'Me?' Thomas was shaking with anger. 'What am I doing? Those songs are secret. What are you doing?'

Weever lowered his arms slowly and watched. Nicky whispered to the cameraman. He nodded and carried on filming.

'Those are my songs,' said Thomas. 'They're Ketch songs. The Wyvern Songs.'

He flung his bag to the floor and stared at his father.

'Well,' said Ted, slowly. 'They're Ketch songs, all right. I taught them to you. I'm a Ketch, too. Remember?'

'But you said they were secret,' Thomas protested. 'You made me promise not to tell anyone.'

78

Ted looked uncomfortable.

'Do they know any others?' Thomas demanded.

'No,' said Ted.

'Don't teach them the others,' said Thomas. 'Please.'

'I promised,' said Ted.

'No,' said Thomas. 'It doesn't matter whether you promised.'

Ted hesitated. 'Well,' he said. 'I suppose . . .'

'You won't, will you?' Thomas begged.

Ted looked more confused. There was a long silence.

'It's a promise,' said Weever, softly. 'You promised.'

'He doesn't have to keep a promise he made to you, Weever. You don't count,' said Thomas. 'And, anyway, they aren't his songs to teach you. He's not allowed.'

'He promised other people as well,' said Weever.

'Did you?' asked Thomas.

'Only one,' said Ted.

'Make him let you off,' said Thomas. 'Not Weever. He doesn't matter. But make the other person let you off your promise.'

'I can't.'

'You've got to. They aren't your songs. They're ours. You can't, without asking me. And I won't let you. Make him let you off. Who did you promise?'

79

Ted looked at Nicky, who looked down at the ground.

Thomas saw the camera pointing at him. He picked up his bag and hurled it at the camera-man. 'Turn it off!' he shouted. 'Turn it off. I'm not in your programme. Leave me alone.'

He pushed through the crowd and ran off.

'Thomas!' shouted his mother after him. 'Thomas! Stop! Where are you going?'

'Home!' shouted Thomas over his shoulder. He ran down the lane by the side of the church and out towards the circle, away from his cottage.

The camera followed him till he was out of sight.

'We'll finish there,' said Weever. 'For the time being.'

'Go and get him, Ted,' said Mrs Ketch. 'Make sure he's all right.'

Ted strode off, after Thomas.

The wyvern weather vane turned suddenly as the wind changed, and faced in the direction Thomas had run, almost as though it was watching after him.

SEVEN

When Ted Ketch could not find Thomas he was annoyed. Then he became anxious with the sort of fear that made itself felt as anger.

'Thomas!' he shouted. 'You'd better come out. Wherever you are.'

He paused, and realised he sounded as though it was a game of hide-and-seek, not a hunt in the growing dark for a young boy alone in the countryside; a young boy who had run away.

He tried all the places he could remember hiding when he had been a boy in Herpeton.

'Any luck?' Weever appeared out of the gloom by the stone circle.

'Nothing.'

'He'll turn up.'

'You're very sure of yourself, Weever.'

'Am I?'

'This is your fault,' said Ted.

Weever pushed his hands into his cassock pockets and walked alongside Ted. 'Have you tried by the pond?'

'Yes.'

'And the barrow?'

'Everywhere.'

'He said he was going home,' said Weever. 'Perhaps he's there now. You could look.'

'You know what he meant,' said Ted.

'Let's look anyway,' said Weever.

Thomas was not at his cottage. Mrs Ketch was keeping cheerful and opening a bottle of wine. Nicky was pushing kindling under the logs on the fire to make them burn up brighter. Her hair dangled dangerously near to the flames.

'You can't just leave him out there,' she said. 'We've got to look.'

'I know that,' said Ted.

Mrs Ketch poured four glasses of wine.

'We need to split up,' she said. 'So we can cover more ground.'

'What's he doing?' asked Nicky.

'You know what it's like when you're young,' said Weever. 'Everything's a battle. There are good guys and bad guys. No in-betweens.'

Nicky looked at him carefully, and didn't like to say what was in her mind.

'He'll not have gone far,' said Mrs Ketch.

'I'm not so sure,' said Ted.

There was a tap at the door. Nicky looked at it eagerly, hoping it was Thomas.

'He wouldn't knock,' said Mrs Ketch.

'Of course not.'

It was Miss Aylmer.

She knelt by the fire and sipped the deep red wine that Mrs Ketch poured for her.

'I did the same, myself, once,' said Ted.

They waited for him to carry on. He watched the fire rise up and lick round the wood. Tongues of flame poked through the hole in a log from the outside of the trunk, where a branch had sheared off and left a curved-edged oval gap, like the opening to a tunnel.

'I ran away. The funny thing is, it was so important at the time, but I can't remember now why I did it. I was about our Thomas's age.'

'Where did you go?' asked Mrs Ketch.

'I mean,' he went on, 'I can't remember what sparked it off, but I can remember what I wanted to do. I can remember what I felt.'

The wind was growing stronger, and it tugged

at the cottage door, as though someone was trying to get in.

'I felt I didn't belong,' said Ted. 'I felt there was somewhere else I ought to be. Not here.'

'We all feel like that when we're children,' said Mrs Ketch. 'I used to think I was adopted, that my mum and dad weren't really mine.'

'It's the feeling you get from fairy stories,' said Nicky. 'Changeling babies, and wicked step-mothers. It's quite common.'

'Did you feel it?' demanded Weever.

'Not like Mr Ketch,' she said. 'Not that strongly. But a bit.'

'You?' he snapped at Felicity.

'I guess.'

'Yes or no?' he demanded.

'All right, yes. A lot. Most of the time. That's why I upped sticks from Massachusetts and came over here.'

'Why this village?' asked Nicky.

'I found it in old letters and diaries, from my family. Way back,' she said.

'I'm the same,' said Weever. 'Always wanted to be somewhere else. Always wanted to belong somewhere. My family lived in Rouen. I went away to school. When I found there was a church here dedicated to Saint Romanus, I had to come here. I knew it would be like coming home.'

'And is it?' asked Nicky.

'Sort of,' said Weever.

84

'They don't think so,' said Mrs Ketch. 'The villagers.'

'I know,' said Weever. 'But it was worse as well. I wanted to go on, to go further.'

'This isn't finding Thomas,' said Nicky. 'We should be out looking.'

'Go on,' said Ted.

'We met,' said Weever, 'Felicity and I, when we arrived. We knew straight away we both wanted the same thing. But we didn't know what it was. We shared information. Old family papers, books, stories handed down. We've both got the same birthmark.'

Together they pushed back their sleeves and revealed a purple dragon on their forearms. Ted did the same silently.

'It was when it started to come through on the skin that I wanted to run away,' said Ted. 'It's the same with Thomas. His is just starting to show.'

'Why did you come back?' asked Weever.

'There wasn't anywhere to go,' said Ted. 'The further I got from the village the worse I felt. I didn't know anything about the gates, or the wyvern world.'

'You knew the songs,' said Nicky.

'They were just songs, and stories. Old tales my dad told me. They didn't mean anything. That was before.'

'Before what?' she asked.

'Before these two came back. Before Parcel came back and stirred things up.'

'I don't think it's like that,' said Felicity.

'Go on,' said Ted.

'I think that what that girl said, the one who went through the gate in the summer, gives us the clue.'

'What is it?' asked Ted.

'There's a new Kych on the other side. For the first time for a long time there's a Dragon Master through there who really believes he can get the wyverns back. He needs them. He brought us all here. I think that it's all over here. In Herpeton. I think that we're going to see something end.'

'And you will go back through,' said Nicky.

'Yes,' said Weever, firmly.

'No,' said Ted, taking his wife's hand.

'Maybe,' said Felicity.

'And what about Thomas?' asked Nicky. 'What will he do?'

There was a sudden crash, and the door flew open, driven by a strong wind.

'I don't believe this,' said Mrs Ketch. 'Thomas is missing in this, and we're sitting here drinking wine. What are we thinking of?'

'I was hoping he'd be on his way back,' said Ted, struggling to shut the door. 'I didn't want to miss him.'

'Well, we'd better get out and find him,' said Mrs Ketch.

'We should split up,' said Nicky. 'We'll cover more ground that way.'

Mrs Ketch put her coat on and gave Ted his. 'I don't mind how we do it,' she said, grimly. 'But we'd better start right away.'

'Shall I wait here for him?' offered Felicity.

'I'll go with you,' said Weever to Nicky. 'You don't know your way around.'

'And we'll go together,' Mrs Ketch told Ted.

'We'll try over by the barrow,' said Weever. 'You start by the pond.'

'I've tried both those,' said Ted.

'Try again. We've got to start somewhere.'

'Report back here in an hour,' said Felicity.

'We can't wait that long,' said Mrs Ketch.

'Give him time,' said Weever. 'Ring the police if he isn't found within the hour.'

Mrs Ketch agreed, and they left the house together, struggling against the wind, and split up at the end of the churchyard wall.

Thomas shivered and huddled up in his coat.

'Poor Tom's a-cold,' he said to Towser.

The wind was getting up. The trees were creaking in the gusts. The sky was black and clear, with clusters of bright stars and no clouds at all. There was no moon.

'We'd better get into the open,' said Thomas. 'I don't want a tree to fall on me.'

They ran out from the woods surrounding

Stone Pond. The wind caught Thomas and bundled him along in front of it, driving him forward.

'Not this way!' he shouted.

He turned, facing directly into it, lowered his head and tried to walk in the opposite direction. But it was no good. He couldn't make any headway against its strength.

'Where did this come from?' he asked Towser. His words were lost in the gusts, and even Towser's dog's ears could not make them out.

Thomas bent double, like a front-row forward in a rugby scrum. He tried to beat the wind, but it spun him round and sent him flying to the ground. He picked himself up and ran with the wind, letting it choose his direction for him. Towser scrambled along, just behind him, his sandy fur streaming out.

Thomas soon realised that he was heading for Parcel's Stones, and he tried again to turn and stop. The wind pushed him over again. The only way he could stop himself from going with it was to lie, flat out on the muddy ground, and let the wind skim over him. He could neither stand up and stay still, nor could he walk against it.

'I'm not going there,' he told Towser. 'I'm not going to Parcel's Stones. Not for anything.'

Towser licked his face.

Small twigs swept over him, snapped from the autumn branches by the fierceness of the wind. Sometimes a larger piece of branch tumbled along, and passed by him.

Thomas caught his breath when he saw a whole branch, turning over and over, and scratching and dragging at the earth, being blown towards him.

There was a crashing noise, and more branches were ripped from surrounding trees.

Towser yelped and leaped up. Seconds later, a branch hit the ground where the dog had been lying.

The spinney round Stone Pond was being stripped of its dead wood, and all of it was rushing towards Thomas and Towser. It was only a matter of time before something large, jagged and dangerous hit them both.

'Time we were off,' said Thomas.

He stood up, and was immediately pushed by the wind again. The only way to keep his footing and stay upright was to run with it; so he set off, higher and higher, always in the direction of Parcel's Stones. No matter how he tried to dodge and weave, the wind pushed him ever closer to the great stone circle.

He made one last attempt to duck out of the path of the wind, but it drew itself into a fist and thumped him forward. He gripped at the edge of the towering standing stone, trying to hold on, to stay outside the circle itself. The wind pummelled him on, forcing him through the gap, and into the heart of the stones.

'Why are you enemies?' Nicky asked Weever.

They were trudging painfully against the wind. Although they were taller and stronger than Thomas, and that gave them an advantage, they were also further from the centre of the blast than he was, so they were able to make some progress against it. But it was hard work and heavy going.

'I don't want to be,' said Weever. 'I like Thomas, and I want to work with him. And I need him, but he won't help me.'

'That's it,' said Nicky. 'That's just the trouble, isn't it? It's always him helping you. Why can't you ask if you can help him?'

'You don't understand,' he said.

'I'm trying.'

'It means everything to me. To work it out. To get the wyverns. To have the chance to go through the gate. I've got to do it. How can I trust him? He's only a boy.'

Nicky lowered her head against the wind.

'He's a Ketch,' she said. 'That ought to be enough.'

Ted Ketch and Mrs Ketch had a harder struggle.

They clung to each other for support against the wind, and they fought it at first. Then, the nearer they drew to Stone Pond, the fiercer it became. Until they were forced to concede and let it push them in the other direction.

'He won't have gone to the stones,' said Mrs Ketch. 'He hates them.'

'So did I,' said Ted. 'I still do. But it's where I went when I ran away.'

'Why didn't you go there first?' she asked.

'I did. He wasn't there.'

They allowed the wind to shepherd them towards Parcel's Stones.

'Not here,' said Weever.

They stood on top of the barrow, the wind streaming his hair back. It was still strong here, but not fierce. They faced into it together, enjoying the feeling of exhilaration it gave.

'Where now?'

'The stone circle, I think,' said Weever.

'I don't like it there,' said Nicky.

'You're in good company.'

'Let's check the house. He might have come back.'

'All right.'

They made good speed.

'I can't see why you're still around,' said Weever.

'Why?'

'A village squabble. It isn't that big a story,' he said. 'To stay this long.'

'My job's on the line,' said Nicky.

'What?'

'I promised them something good. Dragons are

big news.'

'So you believe you'll see them?'

'I'm pretty sure,' said Nicky, 'that even if we don't see dragons, we'll see something just as good.'

'Good?'

'Just as important. There's a big story here, one way or another. And it isn't just dragons.' She stopped and looked straight at him. 'I may as well tell you. I think that something terrible's going to happen here. I want to film it when it does.'

Thomas clenched his fists and breathed quickly. He was terrified of the circle. He waited for the sickness and the dizzy feeling of falling that he knew he was going to have. He kept his eyes tight shut. Slowly, he realised that his stomach was not churning, and his head was not spinning. He also felt some respite from the buffeting of the wind.

He squinted out.

It was all right.

He opened his eyes wide.

The ground stayed steady underneath him.

He knelt.

There was no movement, no terror.

He stood up.

The wind still howled and cried around the stones. The twigs and small branches still raced across the fields.

In the circle all was still and silent and at peace.

Thomas walked to the centre. He looked down at the round, flat stone, set in the earth, with the wyvern carved in it.

He stood on the stone and turned slowly round, looking at the circle.

'If I could walk through,' he said to Towser. 'I know I'm very close. I know this gate could open any time. If I could only walk through, I'd be home. I'd be with the wyverns. Perhaps they'd come with me.'

Towser lay at his feet, contented.

'Thomas!'

His father's voice came ringing through the circle to him.

'Thomas!'

Thomas saw Ted and Mrs Ketch, holding the stone he had tried to grip on to.

'In here!' he called.

Mrs Ketch stepped forward, into the circle. Ted held back.

'Come on,' she said.

He tried, but shuddered when he put his foot inside.

'There's nothing wrong,' she said.

He shook his head. 'I never could come in. Not as a boy. Not now.'

Thomas came over to him.

'It's all right,' he told his father. 'I was the same as you. But I can come in now. It's all right.'

Ted tried again. Again he fell back.

The wind was dropping now. The branches came to rest. Only the smaller twigs were still being carried past.

'I never could as a boy,' he repeated. 'And I still can't. I never will.'

'Come home,' said Mrs Ketch. 'With us.'

Thomas hesitated. He looked back longingly at the centre of the circle.

EIGHT

'What about those songs,' said Thomas. 'Are they still a secret?'

'Yes,' Ted agreed. 'No more songs for Weever.'

'All right, I'll come back with you,' said Thomas. 'For now.'

Mrs Ketch put her arm around him and took him out of the circle. Ted gripped Thomas's arm and squeezed it.

'It's all right,' he said. He looked relieved to

have Thomas near him and away from the stones.

They hurried back towards the village.

The wind was calmer, fresher.

'I don't understand,' said Thomas, 'how you could.'

'Sorry,' said Ted. 'It seemed right.'

'I think it is right,' said Mrs Ketch.

'It can't be,' said Thomas. 'Not if Weever knows things.'

Mrs Ketch kept her arm round Thomas. 'You know things have been wrong here,' she said. 'All year. Ever since Parcel started trouble up at the Manor.'

'Ever since Weever arrived,' said Thomas.

'He's been here a bit longer than that,' said Ted.

Thomas glowered at him.

'And they're not going to get right,' she persisted, 'until we work together.'

'Is that why you're helping him?' asked Thomas.

'I think that if I help him, I'll be helping you,' she said. 'It's time all this was sorted out.'

Thomas ignored her.

'You can't do it on your own,' she said.

'I can.'

'I don't think so. I think it needs all three of you.'

'She's right, you know,' said Ted. 'We've got to

do it together.'

'Why?'

'Weever knows more than he's telling. I'm sure of it,' said Ted. 'This procession. It's important. You can't do anything without him. Not on your own.'

Thomas trudged alongside them, then he took a deep breath. 'How?' he asked.

Mrs Ketch hugged him. 'Listen. I've thought about it. You could be in the procession, and you could sing the Wyvern Songs. All of them. On your own.'

'No,' said Thomas. 'They're secret.'

'Sing them once. No one will have time to learn that,' she said.

'That woman will film them,' said Thomas.

'She will,' agreed Ted. 'It won't work.'

'All right,' said Mrs Ketch. 'What about this? You go ahead. Quite alone. Lead the procession – out of hearing. The rest of us can sing anything, really loud. So that it drowns you out. You sing softly. We'll keep the camera away from you. As long as you're there, and you sing the songs it will be all right.'

Thomas felt a wave of something rise up in him. It was like panic, yet it was pleasant. It was a mixture of fear and the greatest excitement he could bear.

'All right,' he said. 'I'll do it. I'll do it just as you say. We'll get the wyverns. We'll open the gates.'

'Good lad,' said Ted. 'You'll see. Weever isn't so bad.'

'Huh,' said Thomas.

'Well, all right. I was wrong to teach him a Wyvern Song, but I was right to work with him. You'll see. When the wyverns fly and the gate opens.'

Now it was Mrs Ketch's turn to feel afraid. 'But you won't go through, will you?' she said. 'You'll make the wyverns fly, but you won't go with them?'

They were approaching the path that led to the green.

'Hey! You!' shouted Weever.

'Hello,' called Mrs Ketch. 'Over here.'

'I can see you,' he shouted.

They met at the wall.

'You got him, then,' he said.

'By the stones,' said Mrs Ketch.

'Right,' said Weever. 'Now listen . . .'

Mrs Ketch tried to interrupt, to tell Weever that Thomas was going to work with them. 'It's really good news . . .' she began.

'Good news that he's back?' asked Weever. 'Perhaps. But only if he'll let your husband teach us those songs.'

'No,' said Mrs Ketch. 'Listen.'

'You listen to me,' said Weever. 'We've got work to do here. At least I have. Important work. And

I can't be messed around not knowing what to
sing. I need those songs.'

'Hush,' said Nicky. 'There's something we have
to hear.' She was watching Ted and Thomas. 'Are
you all right?' she asked Thomas.

'I told you,' Thomas said. He stared at his
father, and pointed at Weever. 'You can't help
him. I won't.'

'You don't need to,' said Weever. 'Your father
will.'

Ted scratched his cheek. 'No,' he said. 'No, I
don't think so. I think Thomas was right, perhaps. Come on, lad.'

They walked off.

'Now you've done it,' said Mrs Ketch.

'What?'

'I'd just persuaded Thomas to help. To sing for
you. And now you've spoiled it all.'

Weever shrugged and stamped off into the
dusk.

Nicky waited by Mrs Ketch.

'I'm sorry,' she said.

'Oh, it doesn't matter,' said Mrs Ketch.

'There's one thing I don't understand,' said
Nicky.

Mrs Ketch set off to follow Thomas and Ted,
so Nicky had to move away from the church to
keep up with her.

"Just one thing you don't understand,' said Mrs
Ketch. 'You're wiser than me, then.'

'Lots of things,' admitted Nicky. 'But one special one. One you can help with.'

'And what's that?'

'Why are you so keen to help Weever, when you're married to a Ketch and Thomas is your son?'

'I'd have thought that was obvious,' said Mrs Ketch.

'Not to me,' said Nicky.

So Mrs Ketch told her, and Nicky nodded, and said, 'Oh, well in that case, I'm on your side. I'll help Weever any way I can.'

'Thank you,' said Mrs Ketch.

'But it won't be easy,' said Nicky.

'I know that.'

The scares of the night were not over yet for Nicky. She found Henry in the television van, waiting for her. He was shaking.

'What's the matter?'

'I was nearly killed.'

'How?'

'The strangest thing. The weather vane, on the steeple. It was turned to an angle against the wind.'

'Shouldn't it be?'

'No. It faces into the wind, usually. That's what made me notice. It was moving, from side to side. Not regularly, as if the wind was catching it, but just at odd times, when the wind was constant.

It was like it was making the wind come, not being blown by it.'

'It's probably unstable.'

'Whatever. Anyway, I took a camera and tried to film it.'

'Can you work the cameras?'

'A bit. I leaned against the gatepost of the Manor, and pointed the camera up at it. As soon as I got it in focus, it turned, and I swear, it looked straight at me.'

'Rubbish,' said Nicky.

'I tell you, it saw me and it didn't want to be filmed.'

'So it flew down and attacked you, and you ran off into the van and just escaped with your life.' She laughed. 'Oh, really, Henry, this is getting to you.'

'Come and look,' said Henry.

He led her to the Manor House.

There was a mess of smashed stone and modern machinery at the foot of the gatepost.

'What happened?' asked Nicky.

'I heard a grinding sound,' said Henry. 'I looked up, and just jumped away, without thinking. The wyvern fell and knocked the camera out of my hands. It just missed killing me.'

They looked up at the weather vane. The bronze wyvern faced away, ignoring them.

'Someone's going to get killed here,' said Nicky. And she wondered where she had heard that before.

So it was war.

The battle lines were drawn up.

The Harvest Service troops gathered their ammunition of apples and cabbages and parsnips, and prepared to bombard the enemy with them.

The Saint Romanus' Day platoon built its ammunition dump of a bonfire, and prepared its artillery of kites and fireworks, and mobilised its dancing dragon as an advance guard.

And the guerrilla brigade of Dragon Masters, Thomas and Ted, conducted its own campaign of underground warfare.

Weever never left the church locked these days, so the mountains of fruit and vegetables grew in the days before the service.

He ignored them, and went about his duties as though they hadn't arrived.

Felicity chuckled and teased him.

'I hope they've got plans for all this, afterwards,' she said. 'Or you'll have a mess and a stink on your hands in a week or so.'

'I'm too busy to worry about it,' he said. He was tired and anxious. He face had grown thin, and his eyes were bright with fatigue and had purple rings beneath them. 'Anyway, Saint Romanus is the 23rd, two days before the Harvest Service.'

'Will it work?' she asked.

'It's got to.'

'There are too many loose ends,' she said. 'I don't like it.'

'Such as?'

'The book. The key. They're important. I know they are.'

'Thomas has got them,' said Weever.

'But he can't read the book, and he doesn't know where to put the key,' said Felicity.

'Neither can we.'

'That's what I mean.'

'We'll do it without him,' said Weever. 'If we need to.'

Felicity gave him a very suspicious look. 'What does that mean?' she asked.

'Three days to go, to the procession,' he said. 'We'll get the songs from him.'

Henry looked unhappy. He tugged at his left ear.

'I don't like it, Nicky,' he said. 'We shouldn't do things in secret like this. It isn't right.'

'I don't like it, either,' said Nicky. 'And I don't like asking you to help. But he won't speak to me. And I told you, his mother wants us to.'

'It's spying,' said Henry. 'It's worse than that. It's stealing.'

'It's helping,' said Nicky. 'It's for everyone's safety. Remember your accident. And I told you what his mother said to me.'

'I'm still not sure about it,' said Henry.

'If we don't get the Wyvern Songs from Thomas there will be no story,' she said. 'Nothing. Just a tiny fuss over a church service. Stupid Mrs Reeves and her Harvest. That's a joke news item, not a feature story. And then where will we be? Eh? We'll have wasted over a week's work. We'll be sacked.'

'You will,' said Henry. 'I'm just the sound man. I don't make decisions. I just do what I'm told.'

'Then do this,' said Nicky. 'I'm telling you to.'

'If it's like that,' said Henry, 'then no. I won't. Sack me.'

'Oh, I'm sorry,' said Nicky. 'I know I shouldn't ask. But I've got to. If he doesn't sing there will be no dragons. No dragons. No story. I get the sack.'

'And if he sings and there still aren't any dragons?' asked Henry. 'What then? Suppose it's all a flop?'

'Then,' said Nicky, 'we have recordings of a group of unknown, ancient folk songs. That's news. Nearly everything like that has been discovered and collected. A new group of old songs is about as rare as a dragon.'

'So you save your skin?' he said.

'Save my job, anyway,' said Nicky. 'And don't forget what his mother said.'

'Do you believe that?' asked Henry.

'I don't know. Sort of. There's something very creepy going on here.'

'All right. What do I have to do?' he said.

'You're brilliant. Just connect up the tape recorder. One of those that turns itself on when it hears someone speak. Hide it, and get him to sing the songs. He trusts you. I know he does. I've seen him with you.'

'That's the worst part,' said Henry. 'Letting down his trust.'

'It's all in a good cause,' said Nicky.

'Coo-ee!' shouted a shrill voice.

Mrs Reeves was being pushed along in a wheelchair, and was trying to attract their attention.

'I'll be off, then,' said Henry.

'Don't leave me with her,' said Nicky. 'I can't bear another mention of her rotten vegetables.'

'Sorry,' said Henry. 'I've done you enough favours for one day.'

'Ah!' said Mrs Reeves. 'I've been looking for you everywhere.'

Nicky gave her a wide, welcoming smile.

'Lovely to see you, Mrs Reeves,' she said. 'How can I help?'

Ted and Thomas spent a lot of time near to Parcel's Stones.

'I wish we could work somewhere else,' said Ted.

'So do I,' Thomas agreed. 'But it's here. I know it is.'

105

'I think you're right,' said Ted.

They had the full-sized kite almost ready. Ted had helped to finish it, and he had made it from silk, stronger and lighter than the crépe paper.

Ted checked that no one was near before he tried it against the wind.

'We ought to have the ribbons, really,' he said. 'For the flames for its mouth.'

'I don't want them until we fly it properly,' said Thomas. 'On the 23rd, Saint Romanus' Day.'

'I suppose you're right,' said Ted. 'But they're going to alter its weight and its balance.'

'We'll just have to take our chances,' said Thomas. 'We can't fly a finished wyvern till the day. I know we can't. It would spoil it.'

The kite was snatched by the wind and dragged away.

'It's holding,' said Ted. 'The wings are holding.'

Thomas looked anxiously at it. 'It's the legs we need to worry about,' he said. 'They're the weak spot.'

'I think they'll do,' said Ted.

'But why won't it go up?' Thomas moaned. 'It must be higher.'

The kite skimmed the surface of the fields, refusing to rise high above them. It was in constant danger of bumping into the ground and breaking up.

'Careful!' yelled Thomas. 'Tug the string.'

'It's pulling me,' said Ted. 'I can't reel it in.

We'll have to follow.'

'Stay here!' said Thomas. 'Someone will see.'

'I'll try.'

Ted slowly pulled the string in, little by little, but he was obliged to follow the path of the kite, away from the stones and towards the barrow. Thomas was in terrible fear of being seen.

Slowly the twine grew shorter, and the kite drew nearer.

'Quickly,' said Thomas. 'Reel it in.'

He ran ahead. The kite was bobbing nearer and nearer the ground all the time. At last, Thomas was able to grab it and make it fast. Ted ran towards him, looping the twine round and round its bobbin.

'Got it!' he said. He whipped the struts out and Thomas folded the silk just in time. Harry Dobbs walked from behind the huge bonfire.

'Didn't think you was having nothing to do with this lot,' he said.

'Just looking,' said Thomas, stuffing the silk out of sight under his coat.

'I'm doing the fireworks,' said Harry.

'We'll be here to watch those,' said Ted.

'Singing?' asked Harry.

'No,' said Thomas.

'Reckon we might be all right with just the one song,' said Harry. 'But we'd be best with the rest on 'em as well.'

'We've got to get back,' said Thomas.

'Here,' Harry called after them. 'I've been looking for you.'

'What for?' asked Thomas.

'Give you this,' said Harry.

He pulled out a ball of fishing twine.

'Hold a pike, that would,' he said.

'So?' said Thomas.

'And it's light. I reckon as it'll hold your wyvern.'

Thomas walked off.

Harry kept holding out the twine. 'You'll not get it up with the weight of that string,' he said.

'Thanks,' said Ted, taking it from him.

'Mind,' said Harry. 'You be careful. Someone's going to get killed if we're not careful.'

'You mind it isn't you with your bonfire,' shouted Thomas. He was angry that Harry had caught him with the kite the other day and not said anything.

Henry was waiting for them at the circle.

NINE

Henry was looking at a pile of large stones outside the circle. Not monoliths, but rocks and boulders, the size of turkey's eggs and larger.

'Hello,' he said cheerfully.

Thomas tried to smile.

'Haven't seen much of you about,' said Henry.

'You're always with Weever, that's why,' said Thomas.

He turned his back to Henry, so that he could

put the kite back into his bag.

'Only because I have to be where they're recording,' said Henry. 'I'm not working with him.'

'I never said you were,' said Thomas. 'What makes you say that?'

'What are these for?' asked Henry. He picked up one of the stones and let it rest in his hand.

'Nothing,' said Thomas.

Henry walked into the circle. 'Nicky said you don't like coming in here,' he said.

Ted arrived and put the framework of the kite into another, larger bag.

Henry knelt down at the base of one of the large, upright stones. He appeared to be digging. Then he came back out.

'I'll be honest with you,' he said to Thomas. 'I'd like to hear the songs.'

'Why?' asked Thomas. 'To help Weever? Or her?'

Henry pushed his sleeve back, and showed Thomas his tattoos.

'Ever seen anything like these?' he asked.

Thomas looked closely.

'Lots of times,' he said.

'Get away. Have a good look.'

'They're just tattoos,' said Thomas. 'I've seen plenty.'

'Show me a rose,' said Henry. 'Or an anchor, or a heart, or anything.'

110

Ted looked as well. 'There's nothing like that,' he said. 'They're just patterns.'

'Not quite,' said Henry. 'But more or less.'

'Where did you have them done?' asked Ted.

'South Seas.'

Thomas wished he could trust Henry. He liked him, and was interested in his story.

'My dad was an anthropologist,' said Henry. 'That means . . .'

'I know,' said Thomas. 'He studied other people.'

'That's right. I grew up over there. These were done by the locals. Nothing like the tattoos you get over here.'

'They're lovely,' said Thomas. 'I like the patterns better than the pictures.'

'There's one place,' said Henry, 'where the pattern is a picture, if you know where to look. Here.'

He traced his finger down a swirl on his arm. Thomas gasped as he realised what it was.

'It's a wyvern,' he said.

'No,' said Henry. 'See.'

Thomas touched Henry's arm and traced the pattern himself. 'No, it's got four legs,' he said. 'It's not a wyvern.'

'But it's a dragon,' said Henry. 'Wherever you go in the world, you'll find dragons. Ever wonder why?'

'No.'

'Maybe it's just that there are dragons, or were

dragons everywhere. Like to help us to raise one here? I think we need you.'

Thomas hesitated.

'I am trying,' he said, wanting to help Henry. 'But not with Weever.'

'Like to teach me the songs?' asked Henry.

Thomas shook his head, 'Sorry,' he said. 'I can't.'

Henry smiled, rolled his sleeve down and said, 'Well, never mind. Let's hope you get your wyverns flying.'

Thomas and Ted watched him walk away.

When they were sure they were alone again, they sat together, with their back to Thomas's usual stone and took out the book. They did not notice the small click of the tape recorder as it turned itself on when they started to talk.

'What we do is this,' said Thomas. 'On the 23rd, that's in three days we come out here and you fly the kite. I'll sing the Stones Song, this one, and I'll throw a rock at each of the standing stones in turn, while you walk behind me with the kite.'

'Is that it?' asked his father.

'It's all I can think of,' admitted Thomas. 'Listen, remember the words.

> Wyvern Weever
> Wyvern Weever
> Weever wyvern
> Threw the stones.'

112

Thomas sang the rest of the song through.

'The thing that troubles me,' said Ted, 'is that even if you're right, and that's what we've got to do, you're not Weever. Shouldn't he throw the stones? That's what the song says.'

'We don't need him,' said Thomas. 'We can do this.'

'I hope you're right,' said Ted. 'We'll know in three days' time.'

It was like a funeral.

The villagers gathered round the dead wyvern at the foot of the gatepost.

'It could have been me lying there,' Henry whispered to Nicky.

'Yes.' She was directing the cameraman, who was keeping a safe distance and using a tele-photo lens.

Weever stood in the middle of the green and watched the workmen pile the broken pieces into the pick-up van.

'It's like the whole village is crumbling like a rotten tooth,' he said.

'Not that bad,' said Felicity. 'But there's something happening here. Something is coming to an end.'

'The Green Dragon. The statue. And now this.'

'Not to mention Mrs Reeves's leg,' she said.

'That's nothing. Just a silly woman being careless.'

'That isn't what they're saying.'

'Oh?' said Weever.

'They've started a petition. To get you out,' said Felicity.

Weever laughed out loud at this, causing heads to turn in his direction. People exchanged whispers and looked away quickly.

'They'll have a job convincing anyone that I'm responsible for all this,' he said.

'I think you are,' said Miss Aylmer.

'So do I,' he agreed. 'But I can't see it standing up in court, or at a tribunal.'

'No, you're right there.'

'Anyway, I may go before they get the last name on it,' he predicted.

'Through the gate?'

'We'll see.'

'You'll be lucky to last that long,' said Felicity. 'You look terrible. Have you slept at all?'

'Not much. There's too much to do.'

'Is everything ready?'

'It will be,' he promised.

'Tomorrow.'

'As ever was,' he said. 'The kites are made. The fireworks have been delivered. The dancing dragon is finished. The bonfire's built.'

'And the songs?' she asked.

'Song,' he corrected her. 'They've learned that.'

'Why do I think it's the wrong song?' she asked.

'It had better not be.'

114

'Can't you take their Harvest Service?' she asked. 'Just to keep them quiet.'

'I don't think I'll be here that long,' he said. He looked up at the steeple, to the wyvern weather vane. 'Keep the weather clear for us,' he asked. 'Don't let it rain on our bonfire.'

'Why are you asking that thing?'

'Oh, it could tell us a thing or two, I think,' said Weever. And he laughed.

Nicky whispered to the cameraman. A moment later, he panned round and got Weever and Felicity into shot.

'Wow,' he said. 'Good filming. He looks like a ghost. Or as though he's just seen a ghost. What's haunted round here? That old empty house?'

'No. He is,' said Nicky.

Thomas sat in the small bedroom and looked through his window into the night.

The black sky was clear and cold.

The green lay below him, like a battlefield. The grass was churned into muddy tracks by the tyres of the van that had taken away the fragments of the stone dragon.

Deep ruts led to the statue of Jane Gwyer, still lying on the ground, and now fenced off with temporary barriers. Gusts of wind flapped the tarpaulin that had been dragged over her like a shroud.

The wyvern weather vane hovered in the

night sky.

Thomas was worried.

'Tomorrow,' he told Towser. 'Tomorrow we're going to do it. We're going to make the wyverns fly.'

He held the book in his hands, and the great key was in his pocket, as it always was these days.

He studied the book again, still unable to make out anything except the picture of the wyvern kite and the lines he was sure were the Wyvern Weever Song. 'If only we had Thomas Kych's book as well,' he said. 'Then, perhaps we could understand this one.'

The kite lay on his bed, assembled and ready.

He had taken off the garden twine and replaced it with Harry Dobbs's light, tough fishing line.

'Shall we try it?' he asked.

Towser grinned.

'In case it doesn't fly. She might be watching. I bet. She'll have cameras everywhere tomorrow. She knows I'll be doing something, and you can't hide a kite, not if people are watching out for you to do something.'

He tied the knot.

'I won't put the ribbons on,' he said. 'So it will be all right.'

Towser trotted over to the door and waited for him.

'Later,' said Thomas. 'When they've all gone to bed.'

Towser trotted back and climbed on to Thomas's bed, and waited patiently.

Thomas looked out through the window.

Below, in a van parked round the corner, Nicky also sat looking up at the sky. And sometimes she looked at Thomas, sitting in his window, waiting.

She yawned, pushed a tape into the cassette player and turned the volume down low; Thomas's voice, singing the Weever Song. As she listened to it, she checked the words against a sheet of typed paper in her hand.

When the church clock struck one Thomas left his observation platform and picked up the kite. A minute later he appeared on the green.

Nicky turned off the tape.

Thomas started to cross towards the path that led out to the open fields.

Nicky opened her door silently.

The wind, which had been fitful and mild, swirled round, strengthened, and whipped the kite out of Thomas's hands.

He held tight to the bobbin.

The fishing twine spooled out quickly, and the wyvern soared high and fast.

Thomas felt fear, mixed with exhilaration. His heart leaped with the kite, and he was delighted at the difference the light twine had made. But he was frightened of being seen.

117

Nicky held back.

Thomas tried to rein in the kite. He stopped the bobbin feeding out more twine and he pulled the kite back.

It swooped, twisted, and made straight for the steeple.

Thomas pulled again. The kite flew directly towards the bronze wyvern, skewed round and tied itself fast.

Thomas beat his hand against his side in anger.

'No!' he hissed.

Towser ran round and round.

Thomas pulled gently. The kite would not move. He tugged harder. The twine sang in reply, but still the wyvern held fast.

'And if I let go, it will free itself,' Thomas said. 'And I'll lose it. I know I will.'

He looked around.

Letting out more twine, he made his way to the temporary barrier. He climbed over and lifted the tarpaulin.

Jane Gwyer stared blindly down.

He tied the end of the twine to her hand, made sure the knot was firm, then went over to the church.

The door was open.

Thomas could smell the sweet stench of the harvest produce.

He made his way to the tower door, opened it,

and climbed the twisting stairs.

The door at the top was locked.

'I'll have to try something else,' he said, relieved that he would not have to step out and look down on the village from that height.

Towser scratched the door.

'It's locked,' said Thomas.

Towser sniffed at his pocket.

Thomas took out the key.

'Not this one,' he said. 'It can't be. This came from the wyvern world.'

He tried it. The lock grated. The door opened.

He stepped outside.

He was still only halfway to the kite, which was right at the top of the steeple that rose to a point from the tower.

Thomas pulled again at the twine, but had no more success than he had had from the ground.

'It's no good,' he said. He had not looked down at all. 'We'll have to go back.'

Towser scraped his claws against the wall, trying to climb up.

'There's no way,' said Thomas.

He looked out, and felt his head swim. The village was tiny beneath him. He put out his hand to steady himself and found a brick which was jutting out from the rest.

Following the line of the brickwork with his eyes, Thomas looked up the steeple. There, as Henry had pointed out to him, were the footholds, right to the top.

'I can't,' he said. 'I just can't.'

He held tight and dared to look again over the edge.

A light came on in the Old Vicarage.

Thomas gasped.

Weever was still up and about. Why wasn't he asleep?

Towser nudged him.

What if Weever came out and found his kite?

How else could he get it down?

The clock struck half past, and Thomas nearly fell off in his fright at the nearness of the bell.

Go up, and get the kite? Or go down and give up?

Thomas closed his eyes, felt for the footholds, and, before he could change his mind, he started to climb.

It was easy going. The steps had been well-placed. He kept flat to the steeple, keeping as much of his body in contact with the bricks as he possibly could. The steps went round in a curve, so he was facing a different direction when he stopped, and wondered how far he had reached.

He opened his eyes to check.

He was more than halfway, but the slope of the steeple meant that as soon as he opened his eyes he could see where he was, as well as where he was going. He froze. He felt sick. His hands clenched on their supports until his knuckles went white and he scraped the skin from his fingers. He could not move up or down. He was stuck. He remembered Harry Dobbs's voice.

'Someone's going to get killed.'

TEN

Weever paced up and down in the ornate room.
The candle flames wavered as he passed.

He heard the clock chime one o'clock, and muttered to himself.

'You'll be ill,' Felicity warned him.

Weever put his fingers to his mouth, wet them,
and pinched out a candle which had burned low
and was smoking.

He sat for a while, then jumped up and was

pacing the room again.

'How long is it since you slept?' she asked.

'Eh? Oh, I don't know. Days.'

'At least,' she said.

'I'd better take a look at the bonfire,' he said.

'Why?'

'It's in the records. There's always a bonfire. We've got to have one or it won't work.'

'You've got a bonfire. I've seen it,' she said.

'I should be there, now,' he muttered. 'What if he lights it?'

'Come on, Clovis,' Felicity encouraged him. 'You go to bed. I'll let myself out.'

Weever threw his long cloak over his shoulders. 'I'll check the fire. Then I'll go to bed. You go home.'

'What is the matter with you? What's going to happen to the fire?'

'Young Ketch!' he said. 'That's what. He'll light it tonight. I know he will.'

'He won't. He knows it has to be tomorrow.'

'He'll do it to spite me,' said Weever. 'To stop me.'

'He isn't like that,' said Felicity.

'He wants to be in control of the wyverns. He'll stop me getting them,' said Weever. 'He'll stop me going back.'

'You want to be in control,' said Felicity. 'That's the truth of it. You're jealous of him.'

'Jealous!'

'You know you are.'

'Why?'

'Because, somehow, the wyverns are his. They're not ours. You might be able to do something with them, to control them, but he's linked to them. He's the Ketch.'

Weever snorted and blew out a candle, splattering wax. 'All my life I've waited for this,' he said. 'Tomorrow I could do it. If only he'd sing. He's got to sing.'

'I think he will,' said Felicity.

'But where?' demanded Weever. 'Where? Not with us.'

The half hour chimed.

'I'm going to look at the fire,' he said.

'Finish your drink first,' said Felicity. 'I'll come with you. I need some fresh air.'

Nicky stood on the green and looked up at Thomas. She knew that if she shouted out she would startle him and he might fall.

She saw him tug the kite's twine.

She saw him start the dangerous climb up the steeple. With her own terror of heights she was as frightened as though she were next to him. She wondered how he could do it, and she could not see that his eyes were shut tight.

But she saw him stop suddenly. And even from that distance she could see him freeze in panic.

Go on, she silently urged him. Nearly there.

Go on.

He stayed, stock still.

Don't stop now.

Nicky waited, and waited.

She lost track of how long he had been there, frozen, like Jane Gwyer's statue.

She began to count. Fifty. One hundred. One hundred and fifty.

Oh, no!

It was difficult for her to find her way to the tower door in the darkness. She did not know the church as well as Thomas.

She spoke silently to him, all the way up. Do it, now. While I'm climbing the stairs. Get the kite. Climb back down.

Her hand found the door. She pushed it open and felt the night air against her cheek.

Towser jumped up at her.

Thomas was still clinging to the steeple, his head low, his face against the masonry, his eyes shut.

'Hold on,' she said. 'I'm coming up.'

She pressed the palms of her hands against the wall of the steeple, and, for the first time, looked out at the countryside below.

The first shock of the sight was like a punch in the face. It took her breath away. She kept her eyes wide and waited for her breathing to return to normal. Then, keeping her eyes on the distance, and never looking down, she started the climb.

Soon, her hand found Thomas's ankle.

'Thomas.'

'Yes.'

'Can you move?'

'No.'

'Open your eyes.'

'I can't.'

'Try.'

'I'll fall.'

'Hold your head up,' said Nicky.

Thomas raised his head, surprised to find that the tension had made his neck ache.

'Now,' she said. 'Open your eyes, but don't look down.'

Thomas squinted. Then opened his eyes.

'Look at it,' she said. 'Look right out. As far as you can see.'

'Yes.'

'Don't let it beat you.'

'No.'

'But don't look down.'

Thomas could see the barrow, with the dark shadow of the bonfire against the sky.

'Stare at it,' said Nicky. 'It's all right if you stare. Don't let it beat you.'

Thomas felt himself relax against the side of the steeple. His fingers, cold and painful, moved slightly, to resettle him more securely.

'I can do it,' he said at last.

'Good. I'll lead you down.'

'No, I've got to get it.'

Thomas moved higher, keeping his eyes always away from looking down.

Nicky did not follow him. She had climbed as high as she could.

Thomas found the bronze ball that the wyvern perched on. He felt for the twine. The kite had snagged on the claw of the wyvern. It had not twisted and tied itself, so Thomas was able to free it easily. He pulled the twine, and called down to Nicky. 'Can you get this?'

She reached out and found the twine. 'Got it. Come down.'

'Yes.'

Thomas reached out to stroke the wyvern before he left it. His hand brushed against the round perch, and found a gap in the metal. He dared to look. There, right in front of him, was a panel, with a keyhole in it.

Struggling against his fear of falling, he took the key from his pocket, put it in the lock, and turned.

The door opened.

Thomas put his hand inside and drew out a leather parcel.

'Come on,' said Nicky. 'Please.'

Thomas stuffed the parcel in his coat, locked the panel and put away the key.

'Coming.'

Weever kicked the edge of the bonfire.

'The wood's dry,' said Felicity.

'We need to keep watch all through the night,' said Weever. 'I'll stay here. You go home.'

'Nonsense, Clovis. We've come this far. You needn't worry now. Thomas is fast asleep.'

Weever looked up at the sky.

'I can see them, already,' he said. 'The skies, full of wyverns. Again. At last.'

'And you in command?' asked Felicity.

Weever kicked at a log. 'I don't know. As long as they come, I suppose. What does it matter?'

Felicity did not answer him.

'I mean,' he went on. 'I'm going back anyway. When the gate opens. What about you? Felicity?'

He saw her staring at the sky, above the church, at a wyvern in flight.

'What?'

They began to run together.

Thomas followed Nicky back to the base of the steeple. They sank down, and sat together, with their feet against the low parapet, backs against the steeple.

They were safe and not afraid; they might have been against the churchyard wall. They could not look down from that position.

Thomas was shaking. Nicky was panting. She had pulled the twine and grabbed the kite, holding it safe. For a few seconds it had flown up, threatening to escape. Then she drew it to safety.

'Thanks,' said Thomas. 'I couldn't keep holding on.'

Nicky smiled.

Thomas reached out to take the kite.

'This is a secret,' he said.

'Don't worry. I won't tell.'

'But it's your job. You have to tell. You have to film it.'

'No. I can choose.'

'Look,' said Thomas. 'I'm sorry.'

'It's all right.'

'I didn't want to be rude. But some things are secret.'

'I know.'

Thomas checked the kite for damage. It was not marked or broken.

'What happened?' he asked.

'What?'

'To your mother?'

'Oh,' said Nicky. 'I thought you'd forgotten about that.'

'No,' said Thomas. 'My mum was ill, earlier in the year. I was worried.'

'She's all right now?' asked Nicky.

'Yes. She's fine.'

'I'm glad,' said Nicky. 'I, er, my wish didn't come true,' she said.

'I'm sorry,' said Thomas.

Nicky looked up at the sky. 'It happens,'

she said.

Thomas could feel the leather package in his coat. He wanted to look at it, and somehow he wanted to share it with Nicky. He knew what it was going to be, and he was too excited to wait, too sad to leave her.

'I found something, up the steeple,' he said.

Nicky smiled again.

'I can beat Weever, now,' he said.

'Oh?'

'There's a book,' said Thomas. 'Thomas Kych's book. It has all the secrets of the wyverns, and it's been hidden for hundreds of years.'

Nicky looked at him, with excitement.

'I've found it,' said Thomas.

'How do you know?'

'I used the key. That's a sign. And it was the wyvern, so that's a clue. And it's the day before Saint Romanus, so I've got it just in time. It must be the book. It will tell me what to do tomorrow. To raise the wyverns and open the gate. It will make me the Dragon Master.'

'That's wonderful,' said Nicky. 'But why are you telling me?'

'You helped me,' said Thomas. 'I wouldn't have got it if it hadn't been for you.'

'I'll help you tomorrow as well, if you like,' she offered.

Thomas drew out the parcel and began to unwrap the leather. It was soft and supple,

130

like material.

Nicky leaned over.

Inside the wrapping was a small book.

Thomas hugged it to himself. 'It is,' he said. 'It's the book. At last.'

The thick leather binding of the book was embossed with a wyvern on the front cover and a picture of Parcel's Stones on the back.

'Are you going to open it?' asked Nicky.

'I'm frightened to,' said Thomas.

'It can't hurt you.'

'I don't mean like that,' said Thomas.

'Of course not. I'm sorry. I know.'

'I'll be able to do anything, once I look,' said Thomas.

Nicky waited.

'Promise you won't tell,' he said, putting off the moment when he would open the book and have everything he had ever wanted.

'Promise,' said Nicky.

Thomas took the cover in his hand and opened the book.

'Oh,' said Nicky.

'Hey!' yelled Weever. 'Up there!'

Thomas popped up over the parapet and saw Weever staring up at him, Felicity Aylmer by his side. They were following the line of twine from Jane Gwyer to the tower.

'What are you doing?' he shouted.

'They'll wake the village,' groaned Thomas.

'I'll hold the kite,' said Nicky. 'You run down and reel it in.'

Thomas sped off. He ignored Weever and Felicity, took the twine from Jane Gwyer's hand and hauled in the kite. Nicky held it away from the wall to prevent it from getting tangled up again. The wind was kind to them and did not interfere.

Felicity stood close to Thomas, and she helped with the bobbin when he almost got the twine tangled.

'Thanks,' he said.

Weever glowered at them.

'You could have been killed up there,' he said.

'It should have been locked,' said Felicity.

'It was,' said Weever.

'We'd like to help,' said Felicity to Thomas. 'May we?'

'I'm all right,' said Thomas.

'Got your own procession, have you, then?' said Weever, looking at the kite.

'Mind your own business.'

Thomas ran back to his cottage.

The sound of shouting had woken his father, and he stood in the doorway.

'Did she fly?' he asked.

Thomas pushed past him and ran upstairs.

Ted knocked on the bedroom door, waited, and when there was no answer he pushed it open.

'May I come in?'

He took no answer to be no refusal and

132

went in.

Thomas had his back to the room and was looking out of the window.

'I don't mind,' Ted said. 'It was a good idea to test it.'

Mrs Ketch appeared in the doorway.

Thomas gave Ted the leather parcel.

'Look at this,' he said.

Ted examined it.

'It's the book?' he asked.

'Yes.'

He opened it. 'Oh, no,' he said, quietly.

'I'm sick of all this,' said Thomas. 'I just want to go home.'

Mrs Ketch blinked out at the dark sky.

'Tomorrow,' said Thomas. 'I know it's tomorrow.'

ELEVEN

The morning of Saint Romanus' Day, October 23rd, dawned with a grey mist hanging over the village like a threat.

Mrs Reeves rode like an emperor up the church path in her chariot, to check on her vegetables.

Nicky supervised Henry and the cameraman.

Weever, looking more haggard than ever, fastened a padlock to the tower door.

Felicity Aylmer stood in the doorway of Viviper

Cottage and sniffed the air.

'Smells like a bonfire already,' she said.

'Autumn,' said Harry Dobbs, on his way home from the shop with a bottle of milk in his hands. 'Always smells of fire.'

'I wonder why?' Felicity asked.

'Burning out the year. Ready for a new one,' said Harry.

Nicky wandered over.

'Morning,' said Harry. 'Long time to wait.'

'When?' asked Nicky, checking a clipboard.

'Dusk,' said Felicity. 'We gather under the tower at nightfall, make our way out to the barrow, singing the Wyvern Song. Then we light the fireworks.'

'And watch the dragons fly,' Harry chortled.

'That's what I've got,' she said.

'Let's have a look.' He read through her check list, and he laughed. 'I bet that's a first,' he said.

'What?'

'End of procession. Fireworks. Dragons fly,' he read. 'Don't suppose you see that a lot on your bits of paper.'

He gave her the clipboard back and went off.

'Enjoy your breakfast,' said Felicity.

'No time for that,' said Harry, and disappeared into the mist.

'How will you fill your time?' asked Felicity. 'Until this evening?'

'Lots of technical checks to do. Sound, light.

That sort of thing.'

'That won't take all day.'

'No,' Nicky admitted. 'But if this fog doesn't clear we're in trouble.'

'Might clear. Might get thicker and stay,' said Felicity. 'You can never tell in fall.'

Nicky smiled. 'Shouldn't you say autumn, now you're living here?'

'It gives the natives something to talk about,' said Miss Aylmer. 'And, anyway, it's only the old word.'

'English?' asked Nicky in surprise.

'Of course,' said Miss Aylmer. 'That's what we speak in New England. And some of our words are the old English words that you've forgotten.'

'Like gotten,' said Nicky.

'And fall for autumn,' said Felicity.

'Maybe it's better,' said Nicky. 'Something's falling here. And I'm not sure what it is.'

'Pride,' said Felicity.

'Yes,' agreed Nicky. 'And power.'

'And the wyvern from the manor gate,' said Felicity.

The door to the Ketches' cottage opened and Mrs Ketch came out. She looked around, saw Nicky and hurried across to her.

'It's too late,' she said.

'What?'

'They've gone. Ted and Thomas. They've gone already.'

'But it isn't till this evening,' said Nicky. 'We're

136

not ready.'

'Never mind your film,' said Mrs Ketch. 'They've gone.'

'Sorry,' said Nicky. 'I didn't mean that. I meant, I expected them to do it at the same time as Weever.'

'Let's go,' said Felicity.

'Where?'

'The stones,' she said, in her grating voice.

Nicky grabbed Henry on the way past, and he seized a video camera.

'Let's hope we're not too late,' he said.

'I should never have told you,' said Mrs Ketch to Nicky. 'I should have. . .'

'What?' asked Nicky.

They were halfway to the stones.

'I don't know,' said Mrs Ketch. 'I don't know.'

'I've got the song, here,' said Nicky, waving her clipboard.

'They know the song; that's the whole point. You should have got them to agree to do it with Weever. Now they'll open the gate on their own and Thomas will go through. I know he will. I'll never see him again.'

They sped on.

Thomas ran with the kite, threw it in the air and it caught the gentle breeze and lifted.

Ted breathed out slowly, feeling the thrill of the soaring wyvern.

'She's there,' he said. 'Look.'

The wyvern broke through the mist, and rose and fell.

'The ribbons lift her up,' said Thomas. 'They make her fly better.'

'And Harry's twine,' said Ted.

Thomas had to agree.

'With just this breeze she'd never have got up with our string,' said Ted.

They stood for a moment, just enjoying the wyvern.

'See its flames,' said Thomas.

'Yes.'

The kite lifted, and disappeared into the mist, then dipped and swooped and came back again, like a dragon circling over them, looking for somewhere to land.

'Ready?' asked Ted.

Thomas looked at the stone circle. He turned right round, taking in as much of the landscape as he could see in the mist, giving it a last look.

'Yes.'

He piled the round stones into a wicker basket, looped it over his arm, and set off round the stones, singing in a clear, pure voice. As he passed each tall stone he threw a rock at it.

'Wyvern Weever
Wyvern Weever

Weever wyvern
Threw the stones.'

The clash of the rock against the stones rang
out, quietly at first, then louder and louder, as
though each sound did not fade away, but
lived on and joined with the next, in a growing
chord.

'Fly, wyvern, fly
Through the night.
Darken the sky
With deadly flight.'

Clash!
Ted followed with the kite, holding it steady
against the now-growing breeze.

'Sail, wyvern, sail
Through the sky.
Flourish your tail
As clouds go by.'

Clash!
The stones rang out, with ever growing noise,
like the engine of a great machine, revving up.

Mrs Ketch stopped and listened.
'What's that?' she said.
'It's terrible,' said Nicky. 'Like a lion, dying.'
'Or a dragon coming back to life,' said Felicity.
'Come on.'

They were halfway round. Thomas was growing more and more nervous. The reverberations of the sound were eating into him, making him falter in his singing.

> 'Burn, wyvern, burn
> In the deep earth's heart.
> Turn, wyvern, turn
> When dangers start.'

The basket was growing lighter now. The rocks nearly all gone.

'Thomas!'

His mother's voice made him stumble.

'Thomas!'

He hurried up, walking faster, singing more quickly, throwing the rocks more frantically.

> 'Wyvern, return
> Through ages long,
> When we learn
> The wyvern song.
>
> Wyvern Weever
> Wyvern Weever
> Weever wyvern
> Threw the stones.

'There!'

The song was finished. Every rock had been thrown. The stones were singing out in reply.

Thomas looked desperately up at the grey sky.

'Come on!' he said. 'Where are you? Come on!'

Ted steadied the kite and looked up with him.

'They're not coming,' he said.

'Into the circle! Quick!'

'No, I can't,' said Ted.

'You've got to. Now!'

Thomas dragged Ted inside the ring of stones.

The echoing sound was louder there, more penetrating.

They looked up.

The sky had gone.

The stones seemed to throw out branches and meet overhead, making a ceiling.

It was dark and clear, no more mist. They were in a great chamber.

Above their heads a wyvern swooped and fell.

Thomas ducked so that it would miss him, and his eye caught sight of three people – a boy in a grey robe, a huge man with a black beard and wild eyes, and a girl.

Thomas walked towards them.

'Thomas!'

Mrs Ketch watched in disbelief as Ted and Thomas disappeared in the circle.

One moment they were there. The next, they had gone.

'Come back!'

She ran in after them.

The echoes died down. The darkness cleared. The stones drew back their arms and settled themselves back into place.

The wyvern turned back into a kite on the end of a line of twine.

The mist swirled round them.

'Thomas!'

Mrs Ketch hurled herself at him.

'Are you all right?'

'They were here,' said Thomas. 'We were in the wyvern world. They were waiting for us.'

Henry fumbled with the camera, trying to make it work.

'Thank God, you're safe,' said Mrs Ketch.

'Did you see it?' asked Ted. 'Did you see the wyvern?'

'No,' said Nicky. 'You vanished for a few seconds, but it might be that you just stepped out of sight behind a stone. It might have been the mist.'

'You ruined it,' said Thomas. 'You spoiled it. You stopped it working.'

'No,' said Ted.

'We were there,' said Thomas.

'No, I don't think so. We made a gap. We didn't open a gate. We were doing something wrong.'

'No,' said Thomas.

'You know we weren't there,' said his father. 'We just caught a glimpse. If we'd had the book we might have done it properly. If it hadn't been ruined.'

'What's that?' asked Felicity, who had been paying keen attention.

'Well?' asked Ted.

'She might as well know,' said Thomas.

He told her about finding the book, hidden in the base of the weather vane.

'Ruined?' she said.

Thomas took the book from his jacket.

Felicity turned the pages. They were eaten by insects, damaged by water and the choking heat that had been gathered through years of summers in the globe. A few words here and there, recognisable as English, a diagram, a picture from time to time were all that was left.

'It's exactly the same as the book that came through from the wyvern world,' Ted explained. 'The few pages that are left correspond exactly.'

'So we would have understood after all,' said Felicity sadly. 'It was all there.'

'Yes,' said Ted. 'Even about the Black Bairn. Now we'll never know where she fits in.'

'She did her job,' said Felicity, remembering Franny, the black girl who had travelled to the wyvern world and brought back the book and the key, and the bottle that had made Mrs Ketch well again.

'But I don't understand where she fits in,' he said.

'Why should you?' said Felicity. 'It's only in

books that everything's neat and tidy. This is real life.'

'I'd like to know, though,' said Ted.

'So would I,' she admitted. 'Maybe one day. I'll tell you a secret, though. I knew a little bit about her. Before she appeared.'

'How?' asked Ted.

'Thomas spotted it. In the book. It said Blaceberian. I was so excited when we discovered it. I told him it was a recipe for blackberry jam, but I knew it wasn't. In my family we've always talked about the Black Bairn. So I expected to see her one day.'

'The books. They hide more than they tell. But it was our one chance,' said Ted. 'And it didn't work. Now we'll never do it. Now the book's lost.'

'You could try Weever's way, tonight,' said Felicity.

'No. I won't help him. I will get through it by myself,' said Thomas. 'I'll work out the wyvern world book instead. If it takes me all my life. There's a Saint Romanus' Day every year. I'll keep trying till I get it right.'

'Unless he beats you to it,' said Felicity. 'Don't forget that.'

'He can't,' said Thomas. He looked at Ted. 'Can he?'

'He knows one song,' said Felicity. 'That might be enough – his way.'

The day dripped miserably towards night. Water from the mist clung to dying leaves, dropped through black branches and dribbled to the ground.

Weever prodded his bonfire.

'Worse than rain,' he said. 'This fog will soak it through. We'll never get it to light.'

Henry appeared with a can.

'Nicky sent this.'

'What?'

'Petrol. Douse the fire with it. No problem.'

'She's not taking any chances, is she?' said Felicity, ironically.

'What do you mean?' asked Henry.

'She wants a good show for the camera.'

'I'll lock it up, till we need it,' said Weever.

'That's right,' said Henry.

Thomas hovered around the edges of the activity. He wasn't talking to anyone now, not even Ted.

Nicky tried to get near to him, but he ran off.

'Are you going to give Weever that song?' asked Henry.

'Only if I have to,' said Nicky.

'When will you know?'

'If the dragons don't come.'

'You're going to show it to him, then,' said Henry.

After lunch the breeze strengthened and began to clear the mist. But the clouds still hung heavy

145

over the village and no sun shone.

Mrs Reeves complained in the shop. 'Still two days to go to Harvest. That produce is going bad. The church is damp. We'll have trouble before Sunday.'

'Now, my dear,' said the lady behind the counter, 'would you be disappointed about that, or pleased?'

'Furious,' said Mrs Reeves.

'That's odd, because you looks pleased,' she said.

'You're all the same, you people,' said Mrs Reeves. 'Just because we haven't lived here a thousand years, you resent us. This village would be dead if we hadn't moved in.'

'You'll be at the procession, tonight, will you?' asked the lady.

'I wouldn't dream of it. And nor will anyone else. He's brought all the people in from outside; the singers, and the band. Except for that stupid Harry Dobbs. It will be a failure. No one will go.'

'Oh, is that it?' she said.

'No one will come,' said Weever. 'I know they won't.'

'Half an hour to go, yet,' said Felicity. 'It's not nearly dark.'

'The light dies quickly, this time of year,' said Weever.

Felicity felt his nervousness. 'I can't think why

146

I'm not worried,' she said. 'I should be, but I'm not.'

Henry looked round the church door. 'Choir's all set,' he said.

'Good.'

'And the dancing dragon's ready, except for Harry.'

'Why?' snapped Weever. 'He should be the first in. Where is he?'

Weever's cassock hung loosely round him, showing how he had lost weight in the last few weeks. His hair, always wild, was now tumbling round his head in disarray.

'I'll sort him out,' Henry promised. 'Got that petrol?'

'I forgot!' said Weever.

'Give it here. I'll see to it,' said Henry.

Weever put on a white cotta over his cassock. Taking a stole in his big hands he raised it to his lips, kissed it and hung it round his neck. It was embroidered with leaves and flowers and winding tendrils, all in autumn colours, and, at the two ends, it had wyverns, writhing in attitudes of submission. The whole work was in silks and gold passing, purl plaiting and spangles, with soft, delicate tassels.

'Let's go,' he said.

He stepped through the door and into the evening.

The churchyard was filled to overflowing.

147

'See,' said Felicity.

'Before you start,' said Bob Marl, stepping up to him.

'No time for complaints,' said Weever. Bob Marl farmed the oldest land in Herpeton. His family had been there as long as anyone. 'You can present your petition to get rid of me when we've finished.' His eyes were dancing everywhere, counting his enemies. No sign of Mrs Reeves, or Snellgrove, or Austin, or their crew.

'Not so fast, Weever,' said Bob.

'Later,' he snapped. 'Clear off, now. We've got to get on.'

'Let him speak!' shouted Harry.

Weever glared at Harry, and he disappeared into the dragon's head.

'Hear him!' shouted other voices.

Bob Marl cleared his throat.

'We've had our differences,' he began.

Weever gave a smile like a wolf.

'But we all want to say, we're on your side in this,' he said.

Weever stared.

'We don't know what you're doing, but this village is special. We all know that. We always have. And you belong here. There's more of us than the new ones, and we want you to stay.'

The crowd cheered.

'That's it,' said Bob.

Weever didn't move.

Bob had a thought. 'Doesn't mean I like you,' he added. 'But you'll do for us.'

'Thank you,' said Weever, quietly.

'Get on with it, then,' came Harry's muffled voice. 'It's hot in here.'

'Ready!' bellowed Weever. 'Light the torches.'

Flames flared up from burning brands.

'Dragon!' shouted Weever. 'Move off!'

The dragon began its winding dance.

'Kites!' he shouted. 'Don't fly them yet, but be ready. Move off!'

The procession began. Faces were ghostly in the torchlight. The dragon and the kites caught the flames and threw their colours out, bright and vivid.

'Music!' shouted Weever. 'But don't sing yet.'

A makeshift band of drums and penny whistles, pipes and recorders played the Wyvern Song.

Weever, at the end of the procession, did not move until the front, led by a wyvern banner, had reached the end of the churchyard wall and was setting off across country for the barrow and the bonfire.

'Song!' yelled Weever at the top of his voice, and he immediately began to lead the choir in the Weather Vane Song.

The wyvern on the steeple followed their progress.

'When the wind sweeps round to the
                              evening west,
She twists with a silent scream,
And she soars and plunges through to test
Her strength against the rushing stream
And ride the wind.'

'Kites,' yelled Weever, and the wyverns rose
up as one, and dipped and plunged above their
heads.

Nicky ran from cameraman to sound tech-
nician, making sure that everything was being
caught and recorded.

'Unbelievable,' said Henry. 'I just never
imagined.'

Thomas watched from his bedroom window.
Despite his opposition he was entranced by the
procession. When he heard the song he felt ill
with anger, but when the kites soared he felt
himself lift with them. He couldn't stop himself.
He seized his own kite and ran out. Keeping his
distance from the procession, so that he could
see it, but not be part of it, he flew his kite and
followed. Softly, under his breath, he sang the
Weever Song, just in case. He felt very alone
without Towser, but the dog was locked in the
house because of the fireworks.

The procession reached the fire. Weever took a
torch, put it to the petrol-soaked wood, and it
flared up, sudden and violent, with a roar. The

crowd fell back, then reformed and waited.

'Again. All through,' Weever told the choir and the band.

They sang the song and walked round the fire.

All eyes were on the night sky.

Weever's face was drawn and grey.

The song ended, and they waited.

'Fireworks,' said Weever.

Harry Dobbs struggled out of the dragon's head and took up his post. Rockets whirred up and exploded into a million stars. Firecrackers shattered the calm of the night. Gold and silver bursts of light broke the darkness.

And all the time, Weever watched the sky.

And all the time, Thomas drew closer to the fire and sang his own song.

The fireworks died.

The crowd stood, looking up.

The darkness drew round them again, and the silence was split only by the crackling of logs.

Nicky made sure the cameraman kept filming.

Everyone waited.

'That's it,' said Felicity. 'We tried.'

The crowd sighed and began to move away.

'No!' shouted Weever. 'Wait.'

They stopped.

'Wait,' he said. 'Look.'

The sky was empty. No wings covered them.

'Nothing,' said Bob Marl. 'But thanks anyway. We tried. And it was good to have the old ways back. Try again next year.'

'Sing the Weather Vane Song,' Weever shouted. 'Just once more.' His face was haggard.

Felicity took his arm. 'It didn't work, Clovis,' she said. 'Let's quit.'

Weever saw Thomas in the firelight. 'It's your fault,' he said. 'You could have helped.'

Henry looked at Nicky.

Nicky stepped forward.

'He still can,' she said. 'Keep filming,' she called to the crew. 'Here.' She handed Weever a sheet of paper. 'It's the Weever Song. Try it.'

'No,' shouted Thomas. He ran out and grabbed the sheet. 'You spy!' he shouted. 'You spy!'

Weever tussled with him for the song.

'Careful,' said Nicky. 'You'll tear it.'

Thomas snatched it back and looked at it in disbelief.

'This isn't it,' he said. 'Where did you get this?'

TWELVE

Thomas stared at the paper.

'What's happened?' said Nicky.

'Where did you get this?' demanded Thomas.

'Sorry,' said Henry. 'I taped you singing the other day.'

He waited for the storm of anger to break from Thomas, but it never came.

'Habgood, my secretary, typed it up,' said Nicky. 'Has he got it wrong? He's willing enough,

153

but he's not very bright.'

Weever was looking over Thomas's shoulder. 'It's about me,' he said. 'I'm Weever.'

'No, it isn't,' said Thomas. His lips moved silently as he ran through the song. 'It was there all the time,' he said. 'And I couldn't see it.'

'I think it's time you two started to work together,' said Felicity. 'Don't you?'

'No,' said Thomas and Weever together.

'Well, as you're agreed on that, don't you think you could agree to use this song. Before Saint Romanus' Day has come and gone?' said Felicity. 'You can argue about it tomorrow.'

Weever and Thomas looked suspiciously at one another.

'Well?' said Weever.

For the first time, Thomas noticed how the big man had changed. His face had grown thin. His eyes were hollow. His lips were straight and tight. Thomas knew that Weever was desperate, and he felt the same sort of fear inside himself.

'All right,' he said.

As soon as he had agreed, he felt the fear lift, and a longing and a restlessness replace it.

'Come on!' he yelled. 'We've got to go to Parcel's Stones.'

'But not running,' said Weever. 'Properly. In procession.'

The kites were loosed again. The dancing dragon reformed. Weever and Thomas stood

154

together at the rear. Thomas flew his kite, and they set off in solemn sequence.

The band played, softly.

Arrived at the circle, Weever ordered them to surround it.

The whole village was grouped around the ancient stones.

'Ready?' asked Weever.

'All right,' said Thomas.

'Please?' said Mrs Ketch.

'I promise,' said Weever.

'What?' demanded Thomas.

'Sing,' said Weever. 'I'll take the kite.'

'Inside the stones, though,' said Felicity.

She and Thomas stepped into the circle.

Ted tried to follow, but as he broke through the perimeter he fell back, dazed.

Nicky pushed the cameraman in, to follow the three of them. But he fell back, in the same way.

When she tried to go through into the circle herself, Nicky felt as though she had stepped off the edge of the parapet of the church tower. She fell to the ground, and lay there, trembling, until Henry picked her up.

Thomas went to the very centre and stood on the flat, round wyvern stone. Felicity stood next to him.

'Film it,' Nicky croaked.

The cameras focused on Weever.

Thomas made himself steady, planted his feet

square, lowered his shoulders and began to sing the words he knew, but had not understood before, until he had seen them written down.

'Wyvern weaver,
Wyvern weaver,
Weave a wyvern
Through the stones.'

Bearing the wyvern kite high in the night air, Weever set off. He walked around the stone circle, moving in and out as he passed each one.

'Fly, wyvern, fly
Through the night.
Darken the sky
With deadly flight.

Wyvern weaver,
Wyvern weaver,
Weave a wyvern
Through the stones.'

Thomas saw the stones of the circle grow dark. Walls began to appear between the monoliths. The sky was growing dark above his head.

'Sail, wyvern, sail
Through the sky.
Flourish your tail
As clouds go by.

Wyvern weaver,
Wyvern weaver,
Weave a wyvern
Through the stones.'

The arched ceiling appeared above him, and
the huge wyvern hovered over his head. He
seemed to see two Weevers, moving in opposite directions, each one holding a banner
aloft.

'Die, wyvern, die.
For ages long
Wait for the cry
Of wyvern song.

Wyvern weaver,
Wyvern weaver,
Weave a wyvern
Through the stones.'

The stones had turned to pillars, and Weever
was still appearing and disappearing through
them, holding on to the kite.

Thomas became aware of another voice, singing along with him.

'Burn, wyvern, burn
In the deep earth's heart.
Turn, wyvern, turn
When dangers start.

> Wyvern weaver,
> Wyvern weaver,
> Weave a wyvern
> Through the stones.'

Torches were ranged around the walls, and in their light Thomas could see a boy, like himself, dressed in a grey robe, singing with him. Their eyes met, and he faltered for a second, but the other boy carried the song, and they proceeded together.

> 'Wyvern, return
> Through ages long,
> When we learn
> The wyvern song.
>
> Wyvern weaver,
> Wyvern weaver,
> Weave a wyvern
> Through the stones.'

The song finished, Thomas was able to look around and take in what had happened.

He was in a huge chamber, round and supported by pillars at the sides and with a great domed ceiling. The air was clouded with smoke.

Weever had come to rest, just inside the line of pillars. Beside him, near to Felicity, stood the other boy, the other Thomas. Next to Felicity stood a girl, about his own age, but just as Miss Aylmer would have looked once.

The two Weevers looked at each other in respect and veiled hostility.

Above their heads was a noise like the sails of a windmill, or the flap of a huge kite.

There was a smell of smoke, and a sense of movement.

They all looked up, and saw a flight of wyverns, circling uncomfortably in the restricted dome of the hall.

The leather wings barely moved, and they swooped like swallows. The smoke from their nostrils promised fire and death.

'You brought them,' said the Grey Thomas.

'No,' said Thomas. 'They were here already.'

'Not until you came,' said the young Felicity.

The two Weevers stepped to the centre of the chamber.

Each now held a banner, with a wyvern embroidered on it. Weever's kite had gone.

'Welcome,' said the other Weever.

Then they stood and watched the wyverns fly for what seemed like an hour.

'What will you do?' asked Thomas.

'I don't know,' said the Grey Thomas. 'This is new for us.'

'I think they will stay,' said the other Weever. 'They are home, now. You have brought them back to us. Thank you.'

'Stay here?' asked Thomas.

'Not in here. But with us. They will come when

we weave them now. As they always did before.'

'I'm home, too,' said Thomas. 'I'm staying. We all are.'

The Grey Thomas looked surprised, and a little concerned. But he reached out and grasped Thomas's hand. 'You are welcome,' he said.

The other Weever looked hard at Weever.

'No,' said Weever. 'I'm not staying.'

'You said you would,' said Thomas.

'I thought I would,' he said. 'But one Weever is enough for any world, I think. Too many for some.'

The other Weever threw back his head in a roar of laughter that Thomas knew all too well.

'It seems we are much the same wherever we are,' he said. 'And just about as welcome wherever we find ourselves.'

'You're never comfortable where there's a Weever,' said the Grey Thomas.

'I'm staying, though,' said Thomas. 'Now that I've found the wyverns, I'm not leaving them. I've come home. I'm a Dragon Master.'

'I don't think so,' said Weever. 'One Kych is enough for any world as well. And, contrariwise, no Kych is not enough. We need one in Herpeton.'

Thomas shook his head. 'I'm staying,' he said. 'I can, can't I?' he asked his double.

The hesitation was enough.

Thomas crumbled inside.

'This is my home,' he said.

160

'No,' said Felicity. 'I don't think so. Not any more.'

The swish of the wyverns' wings grew louder, nearer.

They circled down, falling to the ground like dead leaves.

Their mouths smoked and their breath was hot. Their tough skin scratched against the stone pillars and the rock slabs. Their claws clicked.

Thomas held his breath.

He walked towards the nearest one. It stood, with fierce gold eyes, surveying his approach.

Thomas reached out a hand to touch it. It sprang back, poised for action, and a red flame broke from its mouth.

Thomas moved forward again.

The wyvern waited.

'I don't think we can touch,' said Weever.

Thomas started to sing, softly.

> 'Wyvern, return
> Through ages long,
> When we learn
> The wyvern song.'

The wyvern lowered its head and waited. Thomas put his hand on the hot, rough neck.

'Goodbye,' he said.

He moved towards the edge of the chamber. Weever and Felicity followed. Felicity whispered to Weever who frowned. She spoke again. He

161

nodded, touched her arm and followed Thomas.

They stepped through the gap between two pillars and found themselves on the grass, outside Parcel's Stones. There was a thick fog behind them, and clear air in front.

Mrs Ketch pounced on Thomas and hugged him. Ted gripped his arm until it hurt.

A cheer went up, and Bob Marl took Weever by the hand.

Weever looked pale and gaunt, still, but the haunted look had gone from his eyes.

The night sky was teeming with stars.

Thomas knew he would not sleep.

He allowed his mother to make him go to bed, knowing that as soon as she left the room he would be up and looking out of the window, listening to what was being said downstairs, watching the sky for movement.

He rolled over once in bed as she shut the door, then the next thing he knew it was morning and he was waking from a deep sleep.

The sun poured through his window like wine.

He sprang out of bed, trod on Towser, who yelped and ran round the room.

Downstairs, Nicky and Weever were drinking coffee with Ted and Mrs Ketch.

'I'm sorry about the song, Thomas,' said Nicky. 'Am I forgiven?'

Thomas shrugged.

'It was my fault,' said his mother.

'Oh?'

'Weever promised that if I helped him he would always make you come back home to us. I couldn't do anything else.'

'And your mum told me,' said Nicky, 'so I had to help him, too.'

'Even though they hated me,' said Weever. And he barked out a laugh.

'You got your film out of it,' said Thomas.

'No,' said Nicky. 'Too dark. Too foggy.'

'No?'

'Freak fog in a stone circle,' said Nicky. 'That's not a story.'

'We didn't see anything,' said Mrs Ketch.

'I'm glad about that, at least,' said Thomas.

'Thomas!' said his mother. 'Nicky's going to lose her job!'

'Not quite,' said Nicky. 'Rap on the knuckles, perhaps. The film of the procession was good. We're going to use it to launch a new series on local customs. So, I'm off the hook.'

'I'm glad,' said Thomas.

He realised that someone was missing.

'Where's Miss Aylmer?'

'I wondered when you'd notice,' said Weever.

'We bundled you off so quickly last night, you didn't find out,' said Ted.

'Come on out and have a walk,' said Weever.

It was strange to see the small, sandy-haired

boy and the tall, big-framed man with the wild hair and beard crossing the green together.

Towser bothered at their heels, and they paused from time to time to stroke him.

Thomas swung his arms. Weever pushed his hands deep into his cassock pockets.

Mrs Reeves glowered at them from her wheelchair.

Weever waved to her, and she turned away.

'She'll be up and about soon,' he said.

The sun caught the autumn colours of the leaves and set them on fire.

'It was there all the time,' said Thomas, 'in the words of the song. But I didn't know.'

'Right in front of you,' said Weever.

'It was one thing when I heard it, and a different thing when it was written down,' said Thomas. 'I was hearing "threw" the stones not "through" the stones.'

'Lots of things are like that,' said Weever. 'You only need to make a small adjustment, and everything seems different. Like, where home is, for instance.'

Weever's face was calm now, and relaxed. His eyes had lost the feverish look they had borne recently.

Bob Marl was carting rotting produce down the church path in a wheelbarrow.

'Morning, Weever.'

'Thanks, Bob.'

'Looks like there'll be no Harvest Service. It's all gone rotten. Every last bit of it.'

'Shame,' said Weever.

Thomas gave him a startled look, then saw the mischief in Weever's eyes.

They smiled at each other.

'Will you have the Saint Romanus Procession every year?' asked Bob.

'Should we?'

'I reckon so. I think it's done away with the accidents, now. Don't you? It will keep the peace if we do it every year.'

'Then we will. But the wyverns won't come. We've seen the end of them. They've gone home for good.'

'Maybe,' said Bob. The wheelbarrow squeaked as he trundled it away.

Harry was pitchforking more stuff into another wheelbarrow.

He grinned at Thomas.

'Now then, Ketch?' he greeted him.

Thomas smiled back.

'She said she was staying,' said Weever. 'Said that the girl there was only a girl, and she was an old woman. So it wasn't like two Ketches or two Weevers.'

'What do you think?' asked Thomas.

'I think it's all right,' said Weever. 'No one outside the circle saw what happened. It was all thick fog for them. I think, that if she couldn't stay, then she would have been in the circle when the fog cleared.'

'I'll miss her,' said Thomas.

They walked back out of the church.

The tarpaulin flapped over the fallen statue of Jane Gwyer. The empty gateposts of the Manor left the big house unguarded.

'It's all changed,' said Thomas.

'Everything does,' said Weever.

'Is it all right?'

'They're coming this afternoon to put the statue back up,' said Weever. 'It will look better then.'

'Yes.'

The sun slanted over the fields. Red and gold leaves blew at their feet. There was a scent of smoke in the air. The year was falling around them.

'I'm glad I came back,' said Weever. 'There's lots to do.'

'I'll help,' said Thomas.

'No,' said Weever. 'Don't help. Let's do it together.'

'All right.'

'Welcome home,' said Weever.

Also by Toby Foreward and Michael Foreman

WYVERN WINTER

No one will say when the wyverns of Wivern Manor last flew over Herpeton. But Thomas Ketch gradually realizes that his family is linked to the mythical beasts, and when Towser mysteriously disappears Thomas knows that danger lies ahead.

This powerful fantasy novel, the first in a quartet, confirms Toby Forward's position as one of the most important children's writers today.

'. . . powerful stuff' – *Daily Telegraph*

WYVERN SPRING

Thomas, Jack and Claire are looking for Thomas Kych's book in order to discover the secrets of the wyverns of Wivern Manor. The book, once possessed, gives power to the owner, and the three children are not the only ones who want it.

They are led to Parcel's Stones – an ancient stone circle which few can enter and leave alive. There, Thomas Ketch battles against the evil Parcel in the second book of this thrilling quartet which began with *Wyvern Winter*.

WYVERN SUMMER

Franny and her archaeologist father are
camping by the ancient stone circle in
Herpeton. While her father sets to work
researching Parcel's Stones, Franny goes
exploring on her own and discovers a
tunnel under Stone Pond. She finds
herself in another world, caught up in a
dangerous battle for control of the
wyverns. Can Franny help to make the
wyverns fly, and if she doesn't, will she
ever find her way back home again? Find
out in the third book of the exciting
Wyvern quartet.

Also by Toby Forward

THE TOAD LADY

Tony, George and Steve are spending the last days of a lazy summer holiday together when they spot the mystery girl in their village churchyard. Who is she? Why does she always run away whenever they approach her, and why won't she ever speak? And then they discover that she lives with the Toad Lady — that fearsome old woman whom they think is a witch! Tony bravely decides to explore further and makes some startling discoveries.